CW01500346

CHAPTER ONE

One thing I can say about nearly a hundred years as an incorporeal spirit—it gives a man time to people watch.

I'd spent thousands of hours watching fools make stupid decisions for all sorts of stupid reasons. Oh, they made some good, heroic choices, too, but there was always that one two-faced bastard of an emotion that tripped them all up.

Hope.

Hope promised dreams fulfilled and happily ever onward. But when the shine of hope wore thin, there was nothing left to it but fear.

And fear made people do all sorts of horrible things.

I figured I had a million reasons to be afraid. Ever since my wife, Lula and I had made a deal with the god, Cupid, to bring me back to life in exchange for finding the spellbook of the gods, we'd been shot at by a monster hunter named Hatcher in Illinois and fought strange creatures in Missouri. We'd dealt with werewolves, ghosts, seers, and wild magic, and had rescued a girl named Abbi who was the rabbit in the moon.

We'd fought the god Atë in Oklahoma who had captured Lula and buried her under a house. I'd mostly died (again) and been revived by Death himself.

Our endless trip down Route 66 had become terrifyingly dangerous in a very short stretch of time.

Still, I wasn't afraid. No, like any other fool, I had hope, and I was clinging to it.

Which was why I was sitting at a table that seated three, by a dust-covered window in an out-of-the-way diner in the Texas panhandle, worrying about a birthday.

Lula's birthday.

I knew that sounded small…ordinary. But I needed to celebrate *her*. To thank her for holding onto life all these years I'd been spirit and she'd been half-vampire—holding onto life for me.

"You're staring, Brogan," Lula said.

I lifted my glass and drained the water half down, while she continued to scowl at something outside the diner window. Texas was dirt-dry this time of year, heat punching like a fist, pulverizing the green to dust.

I knew Abbi, the Moon Rabbit in the form of an eight-year-old girl we'd adopted, her black kitten Hado, and our dog Lorde were outside around the corner, playing in the diner's small patch of emerald-green grass, watered soft for playground equipment.

But there wasn't anything worth seeing outside this window except the parking lot and empty street beyond.

"Maybe I see someone worth staring at." I waggled my eyebrows.

Lu's fleeting smile touched down and immediately lifted, allowing her frown to settle.

I wondered if she wanted a romantic birthday, something fancy, or maybe something sweet and simple.

I could do that. Happy to do any of it. But first I had to figure out what she wanted.

She looked away from the dead world outside the window and braced her hands on either side of the bowl of fruit she hadn't touched. "Ask. You want to know something. You've been chewing on it for days."

Weeks, I thought.

I drained the rest of the water, condensation streaking ribbons down the glass as I set it back on the clean wooden table top.

I couldn't just ask her what she wanted for her birthday, because she'd be on to me. Then she'd refuse to celebrate at all because my beautiful, clever wife was as stubborn as a rock in a hoof.

"Think Abbi's worn herself out yet?" I asked instead.

Lu's eyebrows twitched. "Abbi's on the swing. She's trying to convince Hado to accidentally turn on the sprinklers for Lorde."

"She having any luck?"

Lu tipped her head. Sunlight caught like embers

3

in her red hair as she listened to sounds beyond the window. She was lovely, my Lula. Pale and freckled before she'd been turned into a half-vampire, *thrawan*, and even more pale now.

Being *thrawan* made her stronger than a human and gave her a craving for blood, though she still ate food. It also gave her heightened senses, like hearing.

"Not yet." She shifted, the fire in her hair sparking and spreading. "Now, what do you really want to ask?"

I shoveled the last of my mashed potatoes into my mouth and gave her kitten eyes.

"Don't know what you're talking about." I pointed at her untouched food, then at her hands, braced like she was ready for a fight. "Anything you want to talk about?"

She relaxed her ready-for-battle stance, uncoiling by measures as if just noticing how rigidly she'd been holding herself.

Barely breathing.

Not quite human.

She picked up her fork and pushed at the cantaloupe, peaches, honeydew, and grapes. "You've been distracted," she said. "Mumbling to yourself."

"I don't mumble."

"All right." She looked up, mischief in her gaze. "Talking to yourself in a low, barely understandable manner."

I made an offended sound, which earned me a small smile.

"You're keeping something from me." She

stabbed a grape and pulled it off the tines with her teeth.It gave a muffled snap as she chewed.

"Can't imagine that's true." I leaned back and surveyed the diner. It was an old building, wooden tables and chairs, vinyl booths. The walls were littered with farm memorabilia and decorations that involved a lot of cows.

A man with dark spiky hair and rosy-brown skin wandered slowly between the empty tables. None of the other people in the place were paying us any mind, but he kept throwing looks our way.

"I know you," she said.

"Oh?" I asked, thinking I might have found a way to get her to tell me something she wanted for her birthday. "What's my favorite pie?"

Lu's gaze flicked up, her eyes honey-gold, a sunset over soft sand. She was fire and light and hope. Being the focus of her attention made me feel like I'd just found my way home after a hundred years' wandering.

I loved her. Would fall for her again and again, until time ticked into silence.

"Pie." The arch of her eyebrow was a hook of curiosity. "You want me to tell you your favorite pie?"

"How about I just tell you? I like several pies."

"I know you like pie, Brogan. I used to make them for you. A lot of them."

The man cleaning tables made his way closer.

"Pecan," I said, catching at the old memory. "Apple, with cinnamon and clove. You had a way with crust..."

"There's pie on the menu." All her attention was on me now, wondering why I was shaking out old memories like linen on the line.

"Won't be as good as yours. Never as good."

"I baked for you back at Ricky's in Missouri."

This wasn't getting me any closer to finding her favorite dessert.

"You baked cake in Missouri," I said. "You liked that, right?"

She blinked, amused. "Are you telling me you actually want to visit Ricky? Ricky Vargas? The woman you've only just begrudgingly befriended because she saved our lives? That Ricky?"

"Let's say I did want to see her. Not," I added, "that I want to turn around and drive four hundred miles back to Hornet."

"It's only three hundred and fifty miles, Brogan."

"Right. But if we *did* go see her, what kind of cake would you bake?"

"For you?"

"You already baked for me. For yourself. What would you bake? Something you love. Doesn't have to be cake."

She shrugged. "Something easy."

Not helpful.

"Let's say it appeared by magic," I said, casually. "No work involved. What cake would you want?"

"Magic cake?"

"Pretend."

"You want me to eat magic cake?"

"Sure." I leaned forward and propped elbows on

the table. "Any cake in the world. Which would you want?"

She opened her mouth then shut it quick, eyes narrowing. "Why cake?"

I shrugged, working to give off the right signals.

This wasn't important. I wasn't sweating her birthday. Wasn't sweating trying to make it something special. Something unforgettable. Something she deserved after all these lonely years.

I spread my fingers. "Maybe it's just cake."

The man wiping the table next to us snorted.

"Then any cake's fine." The eyebrow lifted again. "Since it's not for something special or anything, right?"

She wasn't on to me. Not yet. But if I opened my fool mouth, she'd know. Then my plan (which was to plan to have a plan) would be shot.

"But if you had a choice?"

"Red velvet," the man said.

Lu's eyes widened. He was behind her, but she didn't turn, watching my reaction instead.

Medium built, he wore a dark gray T-shirt printed with black feathers—no, with crows in wild flight, their grey and gold eyes just a glimmer amongst all the black. There was something about him and those crows, all those wings, all those clever eyes, that twigged my fight, flight, freeze instinct.

Then he turned and met my gaze.

His dark eyes were filled with a universe of power that crackled and glowed. He suddenly seemed more —bigger, massive, made of energy instead of flesh.

"God," I breathed.

Lu twisted to look at him.

"Or," the god said, still washing the back of the vinyl seat that didn't need washing, "maybe devil's food?" He studied his handiwork as if wiping off furniture was the important thing here. "That's *my* favorite cake."

I made to stand, but he shook his head. "Didn't mean to interrupt."

"Except you did mean to," Lu said.

He hadn't moved closer, not one step. But his presence grew, making him shimmer with that heat-wave light only gods carried.

No one else in the diner noticed because the god didn't want them to notice.

We had no weapons against gods, no real defense. Even so, my hand itched for a dagger, a sword, a gun.

Lula's fingers drifted to the pocket watch at her neck. It was magic, but all it could do was stop time.

If a god wanted to find us, even stopping time wouldn't keep us safe.

"True," the god said. "I did want to interrupt. Your conversation about cake was so *riveting.* Couldn't wait to see how it all turned out."

He left the rag and towel on the table he'd been cleaning and used his foot to hook the extra chair where Abbi had been sitting. He glanced at his bare wrist. "Look at that. It's my break time. How convenient."

He dropped into the chair and a waitress strolled our way. She set a huge brownie and a glass of iced tea on the table in front of him.

"Here ya go, hon," she said. "Remember it's fifteen minutes, not half an hour like last time."

"You're the ginchiest, Connie."

She rolled her eyes. "Pulling out more of that old '50's slang won't work on me."

"Not even if I told you it means hip, keen, cool?"

"Compliments won't get you extra break time either." She started back toward the kitchen. "You have fourteen minutes!"

He chuckled and cut off a huge chunk of brownie.

"Since I'm apparently on a deadline here, I'll be brief. I am a god." He lifted the fork full of brownie in a toasting kind of gesture. "Nice of you to notice. Now, let's get down to the important things."

"No," Lula said.

The god paused, the brownie almost in his mouth. He pulled the fork away. "No?"

"You heard her," I said. "We don't make deals with gods."

He popped the dessert into his mouth, chewed.

"But you do," he said. "You've made a deal —*deals*, more than one—with Cupid. And you," he pointed the empty fork at me, "recently came to an understanding with Death that he was very cagey about when I tried to get him to tell me where he'd snuck off to."

"Leave," Lula said. "We won't do anything for you."

"You haven't even heard my—"

The door flew open, and Abbi bolted into the

room. She was a deity of a sort herself, the Moon Rabbit, but she looked like an eight-year-old girl. She wore yellow tights, a purple shirt, and bright-colored ribbons in her thistledown white hair. Her face was lit up with a huge, goofy grin.

"Crow!" she shrieked.

The god, Raven, shifted in his seat and opened his arms wide. "Bun Bun!"

She gave him the biggest hug, tucking her head into his shoulder as he wrapped his arms around her. "I missed you," she mumbled.

"You know where I've been, Bun Bun. Why haven't you come to visit? I have a whole shop full of pretty balls and baubles for you to play with. Oh, and we have cookies now. Good cookies."

She leaned back, and Hado, the black kitten who was her shadow and protector, peeked out from under her hair.

He batted Raven's cheek.

"Darkness," Raven said. "Keeping an eye on Bun Bun?"

"Those aren't our names now. I'm Abbi, and he's Hado."

"I see. Well then, remember, out here…" He gestured to the diner in general, maybe the world in general. "I'm Raven. Big jobs and all that."

She grinned. "Did you meet Lula and Brogan?"

"I did. They are *very* suspicious people."

She pivoted and frowned at us. "You don't like Raven?"

"Should we?" Lu asked.

Abbi tipped her head, taking a moment to consider. "I think so. But maybe not. He does tricks sometimes to hurt people."

Raven stared at the ceiling dramatically. "Ouch, my reputation. Ooch, my ego. How will I ever bear the curse of being a trickster god?"

"Are you going to hurt them?" Abbi asked, serious now, her magic a cool wash in the thick air. "Because I won't let you. Hado won't let you, either."

Raven waved a hand. "If I wanted to hurt them, I wouldn't be just sitting here eating a brownie, would I?"

"Yes," another voice said. "You would."

Standing behind Raven was a man who had not been there a moment before.

The man was big, at least as big as me. His dark hair was combed back old-Hollywood style, his skin pale and unmarked, his shoulders wide. He was as handsome and rugged as a leading man. I immediately knew that was a disguise.

He had chosen this form. I didn't know what he really looked like, but he wasn't a man.

"Bathin," Raven said with forced cheer. "How not wonderful to see you. I don't remember inviting a demon to lunch."

CHAPTER TWO

"Demon," Lula whispered.

Bathin dragged a chair over from a nearby table so he could crowd into Raven's space.

"My name is Bathin," he said, not bothering to offer his hand for a shake. "You're Lula and Brogan Gauge, correct?"

We didn't reply. Abbi wasn't smiling. She wasn't relaxed. Raven still had his arm around her, but the mood was tense.

"Why are you here?" Abbi asked. "Why is a demon here?"

Raven sighed, breaking the tension. "You know I could throw you under the bus here, Bathin. Demons are not known for being the sorts of creatures to sit down for a chat. It'd be easy to convince them you aren't trustworthy."

"You won't."

"Really? That doesn't sound like me." Raven

shifted to rest his elbow on the table. "Want to tell me why I won't tell them to ignore you?"

"Because Delaney Reed hasn't caught on to what you're doing yet, and neither has Myra or Jean. But if you're going to follow through on this plan, whatever the hell it is, I want to make sure there are guardrails in place—guardrails on you—to keep Ordinary safe."

"You mean guardrails that will keep your girl-friend, Myra, safe," Raven corrected.

"Both, Crow. Both need to remain safe from your wild ass ideas."

"Who is Delaney Reed?" Abbi asked.

"She and her sisters are the people who keep Ordinary, Oregon, a safe haven for gods, supernaturals, and humans. It's a vacation town, and the Reed sisters have the power to say who can and can't stay," Raven said.

"I'm staying," Bathin said.

Raven sat back and grinned. "Delaney really got in your head, didn't she? Big powerful demon stealing all the souls, signing all the lives away on the dotted line. Sitting here in a mediocre diner in the burnt-end of Texas, big mad that I got the best brownie in the kitchen."

"I don't give a damn about brownies, Crow."

"You give a damn about something to be here."

"I give a damn you don't screw us all over."

"Yawn. This would be more fun without you."

"Proving my point."

"Is he a good guy?" Abbi asked Raven.

The god shrugged. "He's in love with a mortal, in

debt to her powerful sister, and has a very high opinion of his ability to keep them both safe."

"But…" Abbi looked between Raven and Bathin. "Do you like those people too? The powerful sisters?"

"Yes," Raven said simply. "Very much. Which is why I'm here—eating the best brownie," he threw a look at the demon, who crossed his arms over his chest and shook his head, "which Bathin wants, but can't have."

"I'm confused," Abbi said. "Is this about sisters or brownies?"

"This is about the spellbook," Bathin said. "We know it's being hunted. By you," he nodded toward me and Lula, "and by others who should not have that kind of power in their hands. We know you've had it."

"We don't care what you know," I said. "We want nothing to do with gods *or* demons."

"Whether you want it or not, you are *already* involved," Bathin said. "Cupid took his god form and fought Atë on Earth. When gods battle on Earth, and you are at the center of that battle, you do not have a choice in the matter."

"You saw that?" Abbi peered around Raven to assess the demon.

"Oh, *everyone* saw that," Raven said. "It isn't often a god appears in full power on the visible plane. The last time was…centuries ago."

"Pompeii?" Bathin asked.

"I was thinking Mt. Mazama."

The demon grunted. "You," he tipped his chin

toward us, "have been noticed by devils far worse than us. Devils you do not want to face alone."

"Gods, devils. Plenty of other unsavory things." Raven gulped his tea. When he set the glass down, he was serious, measuring us with sober eyes.

"If this could be avoided," he said, calm and utterly mesmerizing, "I for one, would be all for it. Bun Bun cares for you. I think Cupid may, too, in his way. This is complicated work made more so by the target you drew on your back."

"Target?" Lula asked.

"Atë. Of all the gods in all the universes, why did you have to draw her notice? She is such an unreasonable bitch."

"Bad word." Abbi leaned back into Raven's one-armed hug.

"Sorry. She is such a vengeful bitch."

Abbi giggled.

"For the third time," I said. "Leave."

Raven held up a finger. "You made deals with Cupid. A deal with the Hush—don't think *that* went without notice. Deals with—"

"We're done." I half stood to leave, but there was a wall of demon in my way.

"If you want to survive," the demon warned, "you need more information."

Lula scoffed.

"Let me guess," I said. "You're going to tell us everything we need to know. For a price. How generous."

Raven's smile showed sharp teeth. "You'd be

surprised how generous a god can be when it comes to the lost spellbook. A lot of unsavory people want it. But we want it more."

We knew gods, monsters, and devils wanted the book. Hell, ever since we'd dug that damn thing out of the broken shack in Illinois, we'd run into more than our share of supernaturals.

And yes, we had agreed to look for the book for Cupid. But we hadn't made any promise we'd bring it to him in a hurry.

What we wanted—the only way out of the deals we'd made and the targets we'd put on our back—was to destroy the book. Failing that, we wanted to hide it so no one and nothing would ever be able to find it again.

"You don't have to believe me," Raven said.

"Says the trickster god," Bathin added.

"But I can be *so* annoyingly persistent when I don't get my way."

"You're always annoyingly persistent," Bathin said. "Except when there's actual work to be done."

"Says the king who wouldn't take his own throne in Hell."

"I like my current living arrangements. That's not changing."

"Not even for power? For adoration? To rule?"

"I have all the power and adoration I need."

"Really?" Raven threw him a look. "Huh. I thought you were just…vacationing from all that."

"I'm here because I want to protect what I value, Crow. I value Ordinary."

"Something we have in common," Raven said. "So do you want the information or not?" he asked us.

I opened my mouth to tell him to shove off.

"What does it cost?" Lula asked.

"This," he said. "Your time. Your willingness to listen."

The diner song changed to Kenny Rogers talking about poker hands—when to fold 'em. When to hold 'em.

If we listened to whatever information he wanted to give us, I knew someday we'd owe this god more than our time. Listening would be a terrible idea.

"Tell us," Lula said.

I stifled a sigh. This was not going to end well.

Raven put his fork down.

"The gods' spellbook has been forgotten by many. By most. An experiment lost to the dust of time. Now it's reappeared, but it is not easy to keep. You know that.

"The book won't allow just anyone to handle it. It also won't allow just anyone to speak the spells within it to wield the gods' magic. You've touched it. One of you." He narrowed his eyes at me. "Brogan?"

"I touched it, and it knocked me on my ass."

The smile again, with just the hint of tooth. "So, Lula, you're the one who can hold it."

Her head made the smallest motion of refusal, then stopped. "Back in McLean. I had it in my hands."

"What happened?" Raven asked.

17

"A monster hunter." It was her turn to show a little teeth. "With a gun. He took it."

"Was he human?" Bathin asked.

"Does it matter?" I asked.

"Yes," the demon said.

I made a short list of the people I knew who had touched the book: Stella who had hidden it in the little shack before she'd become a ghost. Hatcher, the monster hunter with the gun, who had stolen it. Lula, me. And Atë.

The only one of that bunch who had been purely human was Stella. But now that I thought about it, there was a chance she had supernatural in her blood and didn't know it.

"Hands and voice," Raven went on like he'd given this lecture a hundred times. "It takes two beings to use the book. One to hold it, the other to speak the spells. It was a safety feature, I think. I don't remember who made it that way. One of the goodie-good gods, I'm sure."

"That's the information you thought we needed?" I asked. "That it takes two not-quite-humans to use the book?"

"Two not-quite-humans like you," Raven said. "Exactly like you. *Exclusively* like you."

His words punched the oxygen out of the place. And the hits kept coming.

"It's why Atë tried to kill you, Brogan, and hold you, Lula. It's why you were attacked a hundred years ago. It's why your souls were shredded and a piece of each of your souls was stitched into the other. It's why you were chained to the earth. To follow Route 66 so Atë could keep an eye on you.

"You were born for this, and then you were *made* into this so Atë could find the book, keep the book, and use the book."

I slipped my hand over Lula's beneath the table. The ice of her skin stung against the heat of my palm.

"I don't know why you two were chosen," Raven said, as if we were talking about a shopping list, how the crops were coming in, if it were going to rain.

"It's their souls," Bathin said. "And their love."

My hand clenched. What did a demon know about love?

Bathin grunted, reading my reaction. "Demons make the human soul our specialty—mostly to exploit it. It's why we know the power of love. How it can destroy and be destroyed, how it can survive and even thrive against all hope."

"So, there you have it," Raven said. "Your souls and love have made you targets. Along with your stubbornness. Congrats.

"This is me putting all the cards I can on the table." He spread his fingers across the table top like he was revealing a winning hand. "You need to find the spell book. Out of all the options, I'd rather have it in your hands than any of the others who want it and will use it."

He leaned back. "I will help you in any way I can —without crossing the deals you have made with Cupid, and without him knowing, if that's how you want to play it."

"Generous." My voice was distant in my ears. Shock, I thought.

"Not generous," he corrected. "I'm offering to help you for very selfish reasons. That book is a terrible mistake. It's a fucking universe-ending bomb waiting to go off. Gods are arrogant. They think they are untouchable, unbeatable. Unkillable."

Abbi made a little sound indicating she agreed.

"Creating a book of magic, one spell from each god, might have been a lark, an experiment, long forgotten. But for those of us who still kick around this earthly plane? It is an absolute shit show about to happen."

"Shit show already happened," Bathin said.

"Because Cupid and Atë fought?" Abbi asked.

Raven tightened his arm around her. "More than that, Bun Bun. Did you hear the ruckus in the Underworld?"

"The King falling?"

He nodded.

"There was a dragon too," Abbi said as if remembering something she'd seen in dreams. "Was the dragon a spell in the book?"

"No, that was Delaney's angry pet. But the whole reason the showdown happened was because the Demon King tore a page out of the book and used the spell. If a demon can figure out a loophole to get his hands on that power, then anything can figure out a loophole."

Bathin crossed arms over his chest again.

"Demons and worse are looking for the spellbook. Hunting for it. They're hunting the two of you too."

"Because I can touch it?" Lula asked.

"Yes," Raven said. "And because when you hold it, Brogan could cast every one of those powerful spells in it."

CHAPTER THREE

Kenny was done singing about his poker game, and now Jerry Lee Lewis wasn't faking about all the shaking.

Jerry wasn't the only one shaking. Raven's words were an earthquake, juddering solid ground out from under me, tumbling logic down into the rubble of old fears.

I didn't want to believe him.

Lula could touch the book. I understood that. I'd seen it with my own eyes. But that I could wield the magic of the gods? That I could wield the power of the gods?

No. That had to be a lie.

"Bullshit," I said. "You come here, find us licking our wounds, make nice with Abbi, and then tell us *we're* the problem? Fucking horseshit."

The god blinked. "You are not the problem. You are in fact, the only damn solution I can see."

"What solution?" Lula squeezed my hand to calm me.

"Yes, Crow," Bathin challenged, turning his way. "What's this easy solution you've dreamed up?"

"I didn't say it would be easy. But it's the only way I see this not ending in destruction. Brogan and Lula must find the book and take it somewhere safe. Somewhere out of the reach of demons, immortals, gods, or anything else that wants it."

"Sure," Bathin said. "Easy. Except there is no safe place."

"There is."

"Where? With you?"

Raven tapped a finger on the table. "*I* don't want it. And no other god should have it either. Including Atë. Including Cupid. It draws attention and creates chaos."

"Puts you out of a job," Bathin muttered.

"Puts too many people I care for in danger," Raven said pointedly.

Bathin sniffed but didn't argue.

"Get the book," Raven said. "Just like you promised Cupid you would. But instead of giving it to him, or keeping it for yourself, or, hell, selling it or whatever else you might have decided to do with it, bring it to the one place in the world where it will be safe, untouched, unused, and will actually remain hidden."

There it was. He was just the same as any of the other gods. He wanted control over the book.

"Where is this safe place?" Lula asked.

"A small town most people drive through without stopping. A place gods cannot meddle with, cannot change, cannot enter without getting approval from the woman who guards it. A woman with the power to block gods and monsters from entering."

"Where is this mystical Brigadoon?" I asked.

"Oregon," he said. "A town called Ordinary."

"Where the gods vacation?" Lu asked.

He nodded. "Gods put down their power to live there as humans. Supernaturals stay there too. Everyone follows human laws. We even have a handful of demons who haven't gotten themselves kicked out yet."

Bathin shook his head. "It's...one of the safest places I can think of to keep something as powerful as the book. You're thinking of Myra's library?"

"That was my first thought. She'll keep it, I know that. But it might put her at risk too."

"No one can find the library without her," Bathin said. "No one can open it but her, and she has to do it willingly. She doesn't let anyone in."

"Well, except Than," Raven said.

Bathin shrugged. "It's his love of tea and literature that won her over."

"C'mon. All the Reed sisters adore him."

"Who is Than?" Lu asked.

"Is he Death?" I asked. Images of the near-death I'd recently experienced, of the god, Death, in a shirt with a map of Oregon on it came back to me.

He had told me he was on vacation, and therefore

refused to accept my death. He had sent me back to life instead.

Back to save Lula from Atë.

"He is the god of death," Raven said.

"Is Myra a powerful sister?" Abbi asked.

Raven tightened his arm. "Yes. She helps Delaney guard the town and keep the mean gods and monsters out."

"Oh!" Abbi said, bright and energetic again. "I've seen her. I've seen them. They're nice."

"Most of the time," Raven said.

"If you don't break their rules," Bathin added.

"What happens if a god breaks their rules?" Lula asked. "If they broke into the town? Broke into the library?"

"They can't," Raven said.

"They could," Bathin corrected. "The town, if not the library. I found a way into the town."

"All right," Raven agreed. "There can be ways a god could break into Ordinary. There can be ways a demon can try to enter Ordinary without Delaney's permission. How'd that work out for you, Bathin?"

"Got my ass kicked." He rubbed at the back of his neck. "And I fucking fell in love which was…not an ideal situation."

"And who won?" Raven coaxed with a grin. "At the end of *all* the shit you pulled, who won?"

"The Reed sisters. Delaney, Myra, Jean. And every single god and supernatural who lives there and protects the town like it's the last scrap of meat on the bones of the world. It's a place with people, with family, like no other on this earth."

"Truth," Raven said. "Bring it to Ordinary. I promise it will be safe."

"We don't have the book," I said. "We don't have any idea where it is. And I'm not promising either of you shit."

"Reasonable," Raven said. "I hate making deals with gods too. Just…think about it, okay?" He turned his attention to Lula, raised an eyebrow waiting for her agreement.

She held so still, she wasn't even breathing.

I wondered if she was going to haggle with him. Ask for something, like the continuing of our lives, a cure for her half-vampirism, or the whereabout of the monsters who had attacked us and made me spirit and her *thrawan* all those years ago.

I squeezed her hand, letting her know if she wanted to make another deal, I'd be there with her, no matter the price we had to pay.

She squeezed back and exhaled, remaining silent.

"All right then." Raven's fingertips fell into a blunt rhythm on the tabletop.

The sound of the diner came flooding back, the hiss of meat on the grill, soft chatter, the trill of John Denver singing about country roads taking him home.

I hadn't realized the world had gone a little foggy, a little distant while we'd been talking, until now.

Gods.

"I'll get out of your way," Raven continued. "But if you need anything…"

"With no strings attached," Abbi added.

"…with no strings attached." Raven gave her the stink eye. "Where's the trust? Call on me." He placed a single glossy black feather on the table.

"Or me." Bathin placed a small object the size of a walnut next to the feather.

It was a stone, white with spots of black and a slight opalescent shine over pewter shadow.

"Oh." Abbi reached for it, paused to glance at Bathin, who nodded. "This is a good rock," she said.

"It is," he said. "If you need me. That rock is going to be the best way to contact me."

"Can I keep it?" she asked.

"You can. As long as you promise to use it if you need to." He held her gaze for a moment.

Whatever that stone was (other than a stone), whatever magic or promise it required, I'd find out from her later.

"In the meantime," Bathin said, "we'll do what we can to find the book."

"What?" I asked, startled.

"You didn't think we came here just to tell you to do what you were already doing, did you?" he asked.

I blinked. "We don't need—"

"Of course you don't," Raven cut in. "The last thing you need is a couple meddling devils digging for the gold you promised Cupid. We won't get in your way. You have my word."

He placed his hand over his heart and gave me what I assumed he thought was an innocent look.

"When we find a lead on it…" Bathin said, rising from the chair.

"If," Raven added, giving Abbi a little kiss on the top of her head. "Come see me, Bun Bun," he whispered. "It will be fun."

"*When* we find a lead," the demon insisted, "we will contact you."

"Through the stone and feather?" I asked. "That sounds like something we don't need."

The demon shrugged. "Throw them both away. It didn't take a feather or stone to find you here."

"I'm keeping the rock," Abbi insisted. "I like it."

"Hey, what about the feather?" Raven asked.

"I'll give it to Hado. He can eat it." As if he'd been summoned, the little black cat popped his head out of the backpack she wore and mewled.

Raven chuckled. "Gasp, I say. Don't eat it, but yes, he can have it."

Hado clambered up out of the pack, balanced on her shoulder and leaped gracefully onto the table, landing directly on the feather. The cat batted it, bit it, and growled a tiny growl.

Abbi laughed.

Raven stood. "Well, I can see how I rate around here." He turned and gave Abbi a full hug, which she returned. "Be careful and be *smart*, Bun Bun. I'll do what I can to help you."

"Are you back from vacation?" she asked, leaning to stare up at him.

"Let's say no, if anyone asks, okay?" He grinned.

"Or maybe I shouldn't lie?"

He raised his hands like he wasn't going to stand in her way, no matter what she did.

She shook her head. "Delaney's going to find out."

"Not if you and he," he jerked his thumb toward the demon, "keep it on the down low."

"What about them?" she asked, waving at Lula and me.

"If they want to tell Delaney I'm doing a little…*volunteer* work outside of town, then bring them to Ordinary. Say," he snapped his fingers, "they could bring the spellbook with them. Wouldn't that be a hoot? Don't you think that would be a hoot, Bathin, if everyone came to Ordinary with the spellbook of the gods?"

The demon rolled his eyes. "We get it, Crow. You want them to bring it to Ordinary. They gave you their answer. Let's go."

"Some kind of demon you are. Where's all the negotiation and temptation?" Raven started toward the door, the bigger man behind him. "Where's the wheeling and dealing, the stealing of souls and making of bloodshed? Love's made you soft, my man."

The demon smacked the back of the god's head, and I held my breath, ready to get the hell out of there before the fight began.

Raven just ducked and laughed.

"Toodles, Gauges," he called over his shoulder. "Remember, not every god and asshole is against you. I'm the god, by the way." He spun to face Bathin and stepped backward through the doors. "You know what that makes you, right?"

"It makes me sorry I was curious enough to follow you here." He gave Raven an extra shove, which only made the god laugh harder, and followed him out the door.

As soon as the door swung shut, the god and demon disappeared, not even a footstep of dust left stirring.

"Okay." I exhaled, trying to get my heartbeat and breathing aligned. "Okay. That's done."

Lula stood. "I need some air."

"Give me a minute, I'll take care of the bill."

"No, just…I'll meet you outside."

I shifted to stand, but she was already moving. "Lula?"

"I'm fine." She strode to the door and slipped out into the heat of the day.

I stared after her, then dug money out of my wallet, counted it, and left it on the table.

"Something's wrong," Abbi said quietly.

I tugged at my shirt, unsticking it from my sweaty skin. A rush of damp air brushed over my stomach and chest.

Hado pranced across the table toward Abbi, the crow feather in his mouth. She scooped him up, and the kitten disappeared into her backpack.

"Which something is wrong?" I asked. "The god or demon?"

Abbi took my hand, and it was hard to remember

she was not the child she appeared to be, but a powerful deity in her own right.

"Crow's nice," she said. "Nice when he's on your side. And Bathin gave me a stone."

"That's important?"

She nodded. "It's magic."

"I assumed. Is that the problem? The magic stone?"

She shook her head.

"Then what's wrong?"

"Lula," she said. "Something's wrong with Lula."

CHAPTER FOUR

The ache in my shoulders was back, tightness in neck and jaw that hadn't eased since we'd pulled ourselves out of the wreckage of Atë's attack.

Something was wrong with Lula. I knew it too.

"We'll figure it out," Abbi whispered earnestly. "I have the stone. Oh! And the feather. We can call Crossroads, or the owl lady, or Valentine. Yeah! A ghost werewolf will make everything better."

"No," I said firmly. "That ghost werewolf doesn't make anything better."

"Okay, but we have friends. We have friends who can help."

I thought about that. Did we have friends? Lula and I had been traveling the Route for so long, we'd met a lot of people.

But had we made *friends*?

I supposed *she* had because she'd been alive—flesh and blood. Ricky, the Crossroads, was her friend.

There were others here and there along the Route whom she visited. Not a lot of humans anymore. Most of them had passed away. But there were others she'd met and helped or charmed. People who might help us if she asked.

But I didn't know what kind of help we needed. Could anyone help us get the book and destroy it before Atë found us again? Could anyone help us hide it away in a god-protected town? What price might they pay if they did?

Ordinary might not even be what the god and demon had told us it was. No matter how friendly they'd tried to be, I didn't trust a single word that came out of their mouths.

Still, there might be a place—if not Ordinary, *somewhere*—where the book could be buried and lost for good this time.

But that wouldn't solve the problem of us being a target for Atë or other powerful beings. Especially if they thought we were their ticket to holding the book, to casting its power.

I rubbed at the back of my neck.

Maybe that was what was on Lu's mind. Maybe she was thinking farther ahead, beyond finding the book and dealing with it.

Maybe she was looking at our future.

Maybe she didn't like what she saw.

Abbi tugged on my hand, urging me toward the door. "We should go. Lorde is asleep, and it's hot outside."

I let her lead me across the restaurant to the outside.

The temperature had cranked up, lapping off the pavement in watery tongues of heat. The parking lot shimmered with a mirage of black and grey.

I paused in the relatively cool shade of the doorway to remind my lungs how to inflate.

Abbi let go of my hand and skipped off to our truck, "Silver," parked in the shade of a red cedar tree. Our fuzzy black dog lay sprawled in the bed, dripping wet from playing in the sprinkler Hado must have turned on.

I didn't see Lu.

Abbi scrambled up the fender and over the tailgate.

I muscled my way through the heat to the truck. "You okay, girl?" I asked Lorde.

She was part chow chow and part shepherd, a big black fuzzy creature. Dripping wet, she looked half her size. She panted and swished her tail, as Abbi tromped around the bed, moving blankets and pillows.

"How about we get you to a nice, air-conditioned motel?" I scratched behind the dog's ears. She narrowed her eyes, mouth open, content. "Come on up into the cab."

"We're riding in the back," Abbi said. "Together!"

"You can't ride back here."

"Yes, we can." She plopped down on the blankets next to Lorde. "See?"

"Children aren't allowed to ride in the backs of trucks."

She pulled her backpack off and into her lap. "I'm not a children."

"You look like one and if anyone sees you, we'll get a ticket."

She blew a raspberry. "No one's going to see me. I've got a magic feather!" She held it up like a torch, then tucked it into her pocket before the wind tugged it away.

She patted her knee. Lorde turned a circle, then settled next to her, dropping her head into Abbi's lap for gentle pets.

"We like the wind," Abbi said, more to the dog than to me. "And I can help keep her cool." Her chocolate eyes were moonshot, filled with a soft silver power.

The air around them did seem cooler.

Moon Rabbit.

Lorde made a happy growly sound and sighed.

"Well, I want a motel and a shower."

"What about the Blarney Stone?" Abbi asked.

I wiped sweat off my face. "What about it?"

"I want to see it."

"Then you need to buy tickets to Ireland."

Abbi frowned. "Why?"

"That's where you'll find it."

"But…" She dug in her backpack, laughed as Hado attacked her hand, then held up a brochure: QUIRKY AND ODDBALL SIGHTS YOU CANNOT MISS ON ROUTE 66.

"You have got to be kidding me," I grumbled.

"'Stop by the delightful town of Shamrock, Texas, and kiss the Blarney Stone for good luck,'" she read. "We need good luck. Let's go kiss that stone."

"Abbi, that's a tourist attraction to lure people into town."

"So is the one in Ireland."

I opened my mouth, then shut it. "You're not kissing a stone."

"I know. I'm gonna lick it."

"Good luck."

"Exactly!"

I turned, scanning the lot and restaurant. "Do you know where she is?"

Abbi had gone back to reading the brochure, her lips moving silently.

"Abbi. Can you hear Lula?"

She tipped her head and pointed toward the back side of the restaurant. "That way."

"Stay here. No leaving to kiss the stone."

"*Lick.*"

"Especially no licking. I'll be right back." I crossed the lot, glancing in and between cars then considered the layout of the restaurant. I took the closest corner to the back side of the building.

Lu was there.

She leaned against the building, one foot up, her arms crossed over her chest.

The man in front of her was wiry, but taller than her. He wore a white T-shirt, black vest, black jeans, and motorcycle boots.

I knew him.

I'd last seen him in Illinois, when he'd pulled a gun on us, shot Lorde, and stolen the book.

Hatcher, the monster hunter.

CHAPTER FIVE

The monster hunter's necklaces swung, a flash of gold, silver cross, turquoise beads, as he leaned in toward Lu.

I couldn't hear what he was saying. Not over the pounding in my ears. I couldn't see, exactly, what he held in his hand, not through my fury.

What I could see was that he was too close to her —killing close—and drawing nearer.

And Lula was not moving.

I willed myself to be there, in front of her, a wall between them, but I was no longer a spirit. If I wanted to protect her, I had to do it on my own two feet.

I broke into a run. "Hey!" I yelled. "Back off."

Hatcher jerked away from Lula. She pushed off the building, smooth, fast, stopping to stand in front of him, closer to him than me.

As if she were protecting him.

As if she were putting herself between me and him.

What. The. Hell.

I was blowing air hard, the heat bogging me down, the heavy lunch in my gut working against me.

Lu pressed her hand into my chest, stopping me in my tracks.

"He's going." She said it loud enough for him to hear. "Go."

Hatcher lingered, trying to figure out where he'd seen me before. He wouldn't figure it out because I'd been a spirit when the jackass had tried to kill my wife.

I took another step forward, but Lu dug in her heels and kept me right where I was standing. She was plenty strong enough to do so.

"Go," she ordered again.

Hatcher *snick*ed air through his teeth and dismissed me entirely. "Find me," he said. "Or I'll find you."

I pushed. It didn't matter how hard Lula pushed back. I broke past her.

The hunter was already out of my reach, still facing us, walking backward.

A gun. He had a gun in his hand. He took several steps keeping it trained on us, then rounded the corner of the building.

I started after him, but Lula was more than inhumanly strong, she was also very fast.

She grabbed my arm and was in front of me again, blocking my movement.

"Leave it, Brogan," she said. "Leave him. It's fine."

"Fine? What did he want? Why was he here? What did he do to you?"

"Nothing. He didn't do anything." She shoved harder, her hand like steel against my flesh. "Let it go."

I took another step. She made a frustrated sound and moved to the side to let me pass, crossing her arms over her chest and glaring at me.

I jogged around the corner, but the hunter hadn't stayed alive this long by kicking hornets' nests and waiting for the sting.

He was gone.

I could go after him. Chase him down. Maybe catch him before he drove off—

—*pull him through the window and beat him bloody*—

—but he couldn't answer the question I needed answered.

What was wrong with Lula? Why the hell was she talking to the monster hunter who had tried to kill her? He'd had his chance, he'd had enough time. Why hadn't he shot her?

I stomped back around the building. Lula was walking—not slowly, but not so quickly I would miss her—back to the truck.

She was angry. It showed in every line of her willowy body.

Just in case I missed her body language, the explosive slam of the truck door, as she ducked into the driver's seat, clued me in.

I mopped my face, sticking thumbs in the corners of my eyes to blink out the burn of sweat.

A crow, or maybe it was a raven, cackled from the corner of the restaurant's roof. I flipped off the bird or spirit or god or whatever it was and walked to the truck.

The engine was rumbling. Air-conditioning hadn't been a given when the truck rolled off the assembly line, but Lu had the fan on full blast and both windows down.

"Lu," I said.

"No." She waited until I got the door shut to put the truck in REVERSE. "I'm angry. I don't want to say something I'll regret."

I opened my mouth to argue, but Abbi tapped on the window from the back. She smacked the brochure against the glass and mouthed, *please.*

I grunted and smoothed palms across my jeans. "Abbi wants to see the Blarney Stone."

"Lick!" Abbi yelled. "I want to lick the Blarney Stone. For *luck.*"

Lula tightened her grip on the steering wheel.

"It's in Shamrock," I said.

"I know where the stone is, Brogan."

I adjusted the vent. Swampy air that smelled of asphalt puffed against my skin.

"Love," I said quietly.

She pressed her lips together, then lowered her shoulders and relaxed her hands. "I do know where Shamrock is."

"I know."

"I know where the Blarney Stone is."

"I know."

We were silent, the rumble of the engine and rush of air through the windows filling the space.

"What just happened?" I asked.

"You barged in before I could get information out of Hatcher is what happened," she said evenly. "Like I didn't know what I was doing. Like I can't take care of myself."

She threw a look my way. "You don't need to come riding to my rescue every time I'm doing something without you. *I'm* not the fragile one."

I inhaled through my nose, exhaled through my mouth. Counted to ten.

"Fragile." I pointed at my chest. "Six-four and built like a brick house. I'm not fragile."

"It isn't—" She tucked a loose strand of hair behind her ear and made a point of paying a lot of attention to the next turn in the road. "You know what I mean."

"I don't."

"Don't do this, Brogan."

"No, you said I didn't understand. Enlighten me. You don't want me to help you when you're in danger? I know you can fight. I've watched you take down everything that's come your way for nearly a hundred years. He tried to kill you, Lula. He shot Lorde. How am I supposed to stand aside and let you fight alone?"

"I just meant. You aren't like me."

"How? Because I'm fragile? Because my being here, solid in this world, is dependent on Cupid's mercy, and without him I'd be nothing but a ghost?"

"No. It's not…you're not a monster. I am." She wet her lips, unwilling to meet my gaze. "You're human. No, listen. You are. Mostly. More than I am. It makes you…breakable."

I did some more breathing, letting that settle between us. "You can be hurt too, Lula. He had a gun. He tried to shoot you before. You can be killed."

"But I *haven't* been killed. Not in all these years. You have. Twice. And I've only had you back for two months."

I leaned an elbow on the edge of the window and stuck my head in my hand.

She shot me quick glances, trying to read my anger.

"We have gods following us," she said in a rush. "Three. More than three, I'd guess. And a demon, and…I can't, Brogan. I can't see you hurt or dead. Not so soon. Not again. Not ever again."

"This is new." I chose my words like each was a round rock on a pathway and my feet were made of ice. "Me being here with you, alive, is new. It has only been a short time. I understand it's different now that I'm alive. I know it must be harder."

"Not harder," she said quickly. "I want you with me. I always want you with me. But I need you to be safe. To keep you safe."

"Okay." I waited until she had pulled back onto

Route 66, the narrow concrete road cutting through flat land only interrupted by split rail fences and barbed wire.

The windows were open, but even forty-five miles an hour couldn't cool the air, though it did make it damned loud.

"Keeping me safe means what?" I half-shouted over the rush of wind. "That I can't protect myself? That I can't protect you?"

It felt ridiculous to even ask. I was a large human, built strong. I could handle myself in a fight and had done so all my life.

It bothered the hell out of me that she would think I was fragile.

"You protect me," she shouted back. "But I don't need it."

"How does me standing beside you make you less safe?" I asked.

She raised a hand and put on the brakes, slowing the truck. Dust flowed forward, rolling in through the windows and covering the truck in a silty orange film.

"Listen." She cranked the gearshift into PARK. We were in the middle of the road, of old Route 66, at a dead stop. No one was coming from either direction for as far as the eye could see.

"I should have talked to you about this," she said. "Before. Before I agreed to talk to the hunter."

"You *agreed* to talk to that asshole?"

So that's why she'd been looking out the diner window. That's why she'd been so tense. "He *shot* you,

Lula. Why the hell would you agree to meet him and talk to him?"

The other question, of course, was why hadn't she told me she was going to do this? Why hadn't she wanted to do this together?

"He shot *at* me."

"Well, he didn't miss Lorde. Or don't you remember her having to go to the vet to get stitches?"

"I remember." She closed her eyes, then pressed pale fingers against them.

Some bug was chittering out there like bacon in a pan, and a bird I couldn't identify hacked through a short warble.

I watched her, trying to read her distress. Ever since the monsters had attacked us all those years ago, turning her half-vampire, and me spirit, I'd been beside her, invisible, unable to talk to her, to touch her, to keep her safe.

In all that time she'd been determined to find the monsters who had attacked us, determined to kill them. I'd clung to the hope I would someday be alive again and could help her see that goal through to the end.

She'd never given up. Never given up on me. Never given up on us. There was no single soul on this earth as strong as her.

But even the strongest sword can shatter in battle.

"He has a lead on the book," she said, her eyes still closed. "I agreed to hear him out."

Fear, then anger, squeezed my heart until I

couldn't feel the beats. She had met with Hatcher without me *on purpose*.

It would be easy to yell. But I didn't.

Inhale. Exhale.

"When?" I asked, my voice too low. I cleared my throat and did everything I could to hold onto reason. "When did he contact you?"

"After we left Eunice's place. That first hotel."

Days ago. He'd contacted her days ago, and she hadn't told me.

It felt like the world was spinning out from under my feet, and I could find neither sky nor earth.

"How many times have you met with him?"

She opened her eyes. The black of her pupils blew wide, then narrowed to dots in the honey gold of her gaze. "Once. Only once, Brogan. You just saw it. You just interrupted it."

"What did he tell you? What did he say that was worth risking your life for?"

"I didn't risk my life."

"He had a gun," I said evenly. "What did he say, Lula? Was it worth lying to me?"

The world was still rocking, and I couldn't get a grip. I couldn't keep the sound of betrayal out of my tone, my fear overwhelming all other emotions.

…The Hunter. Illinois. The bullet coming at her too fast, and me too slow, even in spirit form, too slow to stop it…

"No. You're not even trying to listen to me." She shifted the truck into DRIVE.

I reached over and wrapped my hand around her wrist.

"Don't," she said, not looking at me. "Don't Brogan."

Her bones felt small in my mitt of a hand, but I knew one of the only good things she'd gotten out of the cursed life, gotten out of the monster attack, was that she was strong. Much, much stronger than me.

"You are scaring the shit out of me, love," I said, pulling my hand away and instead reaching for the wheel. I held it.

Lula made a frustrated sound and sat back.

"I love you," I said, grasping for reason in the fear sloshing through me. "I don't want *you* hurt. Just like you don't want me hurt.

"I want to understand what you did. What you're doing," I went on doggedly. "Why I…why you thought I shouldn't be a part of it. I also want to break that shit heel's neck."

She refused to meet my gaze, staring out the side window, her hands in her lap.

I released the steering wheel. Fear wasn't going to solve this, and anger would only push her away.

I cleared my throat and tried again. "Did he tell you something useful?"

Lula rolled her head and speared me with a look I'd last seen when we'd first been dating. When I'd acted like a dumbass.

"No. Some big lunkhead showed up and started shouting before he could say anything."

I grinned.

She squinted at me. "You're the lunkhead."

"I know."

"You barged in there without a clue about what was going on."

"I know."

"You ruined it, Brogan."

I couldn't keep the smile off my face, even though my heart was beating too hard. I was sick to my stomach, overheated, sweat pouring from my pits, down my back to pool at my belt line.

It was absolutely, miserably hot. Still, I smiled. "Sorry?"

That got a raised eyebrow out of her. "You are not."

"Well, if you hadn't lied to me…"

"I didn't lie."

"You just didn't tell me what you were doing."

She frowned.

"If you hadn't kept *secrets* from me, because I'm so *fragile*, I wouldn't have broken up your meeting."

"This is not my fault," she muttered.

"All right."

Her eyes narrowed to golden slits. "I don't think you understand how stupid that was."

"Following my wife when she's putting herself in danger? Can't say I'd do it any other way, love."

Ice. It was hot as the devil's ass crack, and that woman looked like snow wouldn't melt in her mouth.

"You don't have to protect me from every little thing, Brogan. You can't."

"All right." I sat back. "The same goes for you. I'm not fragile."

She scoffed.

"I'm no more fragile than any other living human man, and since I've died twice and am still right here—alive, if you'll notice—I can confidently say I am a hell of a lot stronger than most human men."

"Brogan."

I ducked my head, trying to catch her gaze. "I might only be alive because Cupid likes me that way, but that is a god's favor, Lula. Even Death himself barred me from crossing the river to the great beyond. That's *two* gods' favor. Not many humans can claim that kind of strength."

She shook her head.

"My body might not be as strong as yours, but I'm not fragile. My soul isn't fragile. Nor is my heart. Because my heart beats for you, Lula Gauge. Always will."

"But that's what I'm worried about," she whispered. "Your heart."

I pressed my palm against my chest. "It's doing okay so far."

She put her hands on the wheel. "It's getting you into trouble is what it's doing, Brogan. Foolish trouble. Just like it always has. I need you to think. To be smarter than that."

"Loving you isn't foolish."

She didn't shake her head, but she didn't look at me either. She just eased the truck forward.

Dust blew into the cab, then back out, hot wind rubbing sandpaper across my fevered skin.

"I love you, Lula Gauge," I said.

But there was too much wind in the cab, too much heat. If she heard me, she didn't show it.

She just kept her icy gaze on the road ahead and her foot on the gas.

For the first time in nearly a hundred years, she didn't say she loved me back.

CHAPTER SIX

Shamrock, Texas, went all out to show off its connection to Ireland. The bars were pubs, the local sport team was the Leprechauns, and every business had green clovers painted in the corners of the windows.

Only a couple thousand people lived in the town, which covered all of two miles.

The single-story, horseshoe-shaped motel where we stopped had Shamrock in its name but was painted in the red, white, and blue of the Texas flag. Huge, single stars were painted on the doors, each one facing the parking lot.

It might not have Irish in it, but it did have air-conditioning.

It also allowed pets.

Abbi settled with Lorde on the couch that pulled out into a bed, the controller for the television already in her hand.

"I like cartoons," she announced, as if we'd never met.

Lu and I hadn't said much since the truck, both of us silently carrying our duffles in and placing them on the bed.

"Do you want to shower first?" I asked.

She glanced at the bathroom, then at me. I didn't know how to fix this. Didn't know what words would make this right, make us right again.

"Lu…"

She picked up her duffle. "I'll be out in a minute."

The door closed with a click. The squeak of spigots was covered by a rush of water. Curtain rings rattled, and the sound of the water's steady stream changed with her movements.

I wiped my face and scrubbed at my hair, grabbing the roots and tugging.

"It's nice here." Abbi pushed buttons, flipping between a huge animated purple octopus and a puppet that I assumed was a blue mouse.

The volume was muted, but Abbi moved her lips like she was speaking along with them.

"It's cooler than outside," I said. "The water runs. There's electricity."

"And it's a lucky motel."

I scrubbed at my jaw, my beard thick enough to itch. "Why?"

"Because everything here is lucky." She spared me a second's worth of a glance before going back to changing channels. "Why are you mad at Lula?"

"I'm not mad at her."

"Is she mad at you?"

"I don't know."

"You aren't very good at arguing. I think she's worried."

I sat on the edge of the bed, facing the door, and rubbed my neck. "It's been years since we've been… angry—this angry—with something the other did. I'm out of practice."

I was also tired, hot, worried.

Stressed, I supposed was the new term for it everyone used.

We had spent a damn long century unable to really communicate. It shouldn't be a surprise that being together again came with some knots to work out.

Back in Oklahoma, I'd thought Lula ignoring her hunger for blood had been what was wrong. But now...I had a bad feeling it was something more.

"I'd just like things to be normal," I said. "To be...easy, I guess. But every time I open my mouth, I'm shoving my boot in it. It used to be..."

"Easy?" Abbi asked.

"No, not easy. When I was alive before, both of us were young and trying to make our way in the world. Then all those years with me a spirit and her half vampire…"

I shook my head. "Not easy."

But we'd been together. We'd done everything we could do to *stay* together. We'd faced every monster, every god, every devil, and always reached for the other, holding tight.

"Different, though," I said. "We didn't…doubt each other. Knew what we wanted. What we were fighting for."

She hadn't said she loved me.

Maybe she hadn't heard me over the air rushing through the windows.

Maybe she was too angry to say it.

One misunderstanding didn't mean she would stop loving me. I'd been trying to keep her safe. She had to know that.

I tugged on my hair again then let my hands drop.

"How did we lose that?"

Birthdays were normal. They marked a time of love, and those who loved you holding you dear. Giving that to Lula, I hoped, would be a celebration of the life we were building toward, instead of the death we'd been living through.

She met with the hunter who tried to kill her. The hunter who shot Lorde.

"Fragile," I whispered. How could I prove to her I could hold my own?

"It can be easy again," Abbi said softly. "All you have to do is kiss the Blarney Stone and make a wish. Then it will come true, and everything will be easy forever."

I let out a breath. "At best, that rock gives you luck, Abbi. It doesn't grant wishes."

She wrinkled her nose. "You don't believe in magic very much, do you?"

"Of course I do. But a rock in the middle of Shamrock, Texas, isn't going to solve our problems. If that stone does have real magic, don't you wonder where that magic comes from, and how much it costs to use it?"

She squinted at me like I'd lost my mind. "It comes from Ireland, Brogan. It costs a kiss and a wish. You need to try it. Maybe Lula would love you again if you wished for it."

The door to the bathroom opened.

No, it shut. Lula was *thrawan*. She was silent as the fog when she wanted to be. I wondered how much she'd overheard.

From the carefully blank mask she wore, I knew she had heard all of it.

I held her gaze. "I want that. Can we talk about this, love? I won't break. Let me help with whatever it is you're trying to get from the hunter."

Her lips parted. For a moment, I thought she was going to tell me what was going on. What she had wanted from Hatcher, and why she'd risked meeting with him without telling me.

I knew it wasn't his death—she hadn't called him there to kill him. If she had, he would be dead.

So why would she put herself in his sights again?

"Lu?"

She cleared her throat. "I'm going for a walk. Alone," she added. "I'm not meeting anyone. I just need...I just need some time."

"All right," I said more calmly than I felt. "Abbi wants to see the stone. Maybe we can all..."

"You can go without me." She gave me a faint

smile that didn't reach her eyes and walked to the door.

"Lula?"

The door was open, heat shouldering into the room.

"I'm okay," she said. "I am." She waited to see if I believed her.

"Okay. But we can…"

"I'll be back soon." Then she shut the door behind her.

The sound of the air conditioner chugging against the Texas heat was suddenly very loud.

"I don't think she's okay," Abbi said in a small voice.

"Yeah."

I wanted to follow, to slip through the walls and drift down the street by her side. I wanted to watch over her like I had for years and years.

She used to want me there with her, when I was a spirit. But now that I was flesh?

Fragile.

I blew out a breath. "I'm going for a walk."

"To the Blarney Stone?"

"No, just a walk."

"To follow Lula like she doesn't want you to?"

"Abbi."

She scrambled off the couch. "I know I'm not a people the way you and Lula are, but I can *see* things. Let's go to the Blarney Stone and make a wish and lick—*kiss*—it and get luck smashed all over our mouths."

She patted Lorde, who was taking up most of the couch, her black fur ruffling under the blast of the air conditioner.

"There might be ice cream too," she said. "Don't you think there might be ice cream?"

"You should stay here, Abbi."

"I want to go. Me and Hado. Where are you, Hado?" She lifted the bed cover, peering under the bed.

"Hado and you should stay here with Lorde," I tried again.

"No." She lifted and dropped the two flat pillows, then rounded the bed and opened dresser drawers. "Stop hiding, Hado."

"Abbi."

"It will just take me a minute—"

"Stay."

A knock on the door cut off her reply. Her eyes went wide, and her mouth dropped open in surprise. "Oh."

"Who?" I whispered.

She shook her head.

"Danger?"

She shook her head again but bit her bottom lip.

The knock rattled. "Hello. Hello, in there," a woman's voice lilted. "Is this a bad time?"

"No!" Abbi slapped her hands over her mouth.

I rolled my eyes and walked to the door. I peered through the peephole.

"Oh, there you are," the woman outside said. "Hello."

She looked to be in her sixties. Her long, curly hair was a mix of blonde and gray. She'd pulled most of it back away from her face and clipped small brown feathers onto the waves in front of her shoulder.

Her yellow sleeveless shirt had the logo of a honky tonk printed across it.

"Brogan? Is it Brogan?" She leaned closer.

She shouldn't be able to see me through the peephole, but she looked right at me.

"I asked Julie at the desk, and she said a tall hunk of a man had checked in, and there you are! I have a flyer. For you. You and Lula."

She dug in a satchel hanging off one shoulder and produced a paper, which she waved.

"Limited time deal. You don't want to miss this."

How did she know our names? We never used our real names when checking in to hotels.

"We're not interested," I said.

Abbi made a little sound, and the woman tipped her head.

"It will only take a minute, I promise. You'll be doing me a favor, really. I don't have to bring people to the bar, but I do have to give away all of the flyers. It isn't a big town, Mr. Gauge, and we overprinted our flyers by a lot." She shook the satchel. "A great lot."

"Sorry," I said. "Still not interested."

"Did I mention ice cream? The best in a hundred miles."

"Ice cream?" Abbi whispered.

"Buy one and you get an extra scoop for free," the woman said.

"Two scoops?" Abbi rocked up onto her toes, every inch of her absolutely straining toward the door. "Ice cream, Brogan," she hiss-whispered. "Half of it's free! I'll share."

"You don't have to share," the woman said. "I can give each of you a flyer. I can give each of you *two* flyers."

Abbi had been whispering. Either the motel door was made of paper, or the woman had unnatural hearing. Supernatural hearing.

"Do you know her?" I asked Abbi.

"I've heard her before. She's nice. I think she worships me." She gave me a huge grin.

"Worships you."

"Or the moon," she said.

"So, she's not a vampire, a monster, a god?" I asked.

"No?"

"Why can she hear us through the door?"

"Probably magic," she said. "Or the door is really thin. She's not bad, Brogan. I've heard her before. She's nice. She won't hurt us. I promise."

I sighed and opened the door.

The woman jerked back and pressed fingers to her chest. "My goodness."

"What are you?" I demanded.

"A local citizen? Well, I work here, but I live up the road a bit. I'm supposed to handle the marketing, but you can see how that's going."

She shook the bag again and it crinkled, paper shifting.

I was good at spotting gods. She didn't have that look about her—didn't have the glow of power. I could identify most supernaturals.

But I'd been spotting them while I was in spirit form, not in flesh. While having a body brought with it pleasures and advantages, there were some spirit-enhanced senses I missed.

"Let me guess. You have an offer we can't refuse."

"It's a bar?" she said. "With an attached ice cream shop? A strange match, I'll admit, but in small towns, it works better when people join together. Don't you think?"

"I think we don't need what you're selling."

"Have you been to the Blarney Stone? The community has done a fine job of setting it up in a nice little spot on Main Street. Great signage. I think you'd be impressed."

"I want to see the Blarney Stone," Abbi said. "And ice cream. Please. We'll take two flyers. Maybe four? Is four okay?"

"Four is wonderful. I'm happy to give you a dozen." The woman tried to peer around me to get a look at Abbi.

"Would you allow me to step…" She blinked. "Oh. Oh, you're…"

I wedged more of my bulk into the opening, hiding Abbi. "Just hand me the flyers."

"She's…um, she's very pretty," the woman said.

I was sure she hesitated because Abbi had darker skin than either me or Lula.

"Is she your...daughter?"

"Family!" Abbi said from behind me. Like, *right* behind me. She'd snuck up and was trying to shove her face past my thigh.

"Abbi," I growled. "Don't."

"Just. Move, Brogan." She pushed, then huffed. Then she pinched the back of my knee. Hard.

"Hey," I yelped and jumped.

She smooshed into the open space of the door.

"Hi! I'm Abbi, and I really like ice cream. Brogan is my family, he's taking me on a road trip, and he didn't steal me. But I really, really do like ice cream, so can I have some?"

The woman blinked and her hand fluttered up to touch the feathers caught in her hair, her gaze cutting between the little twerp and me.

"Abbi," she said, "it is *wonderful* to meet you. My name is Franny. Welcome here. Welcome with *all* my heart."

"Thank you," Abbi said. "Can I have the ice cream papers?"

"Oh, of course. Here." She pulled out a handful of the flyers and bent them all in half short-wise, then length-wise. She held them out like she was luring a skittish squirrel with a handful of nuts.

"Coupons for ice cream. Also, more than ice cream, but if you bring them to the ice cream shop, and Billy is there, he'll make sure you get the best scoops in Texas."

61

"Thank you," Abbi said. She tipped her head sideways and considered the woman. "Do you know me?"

"We haven't met. Not until now."

"Do I know Billy?"

"I don't think so."

"How will he know the best ice cream for me?"

"You can taste each one and decide for yourself."

"That's ginchy. Isn't that ginchy, Brogan?"

"Stop saying ginchy," I said. "Thank you for the flyers, Franny. Good-bye, now."

I shoved the door, but Abbi was fast, the little fink.

She slipped out and stood in front of Franny.

"I think I'd like you to take me to the Blarney Stone. Me and Brogan. Our dog needs to cool off because she's really furry, and Texas is hot for fur."

"Abbi, let's not bother the nice lady."

"Oh, it's no bother. I enjoy showing people around the place. Route 66 goes right through here, did you know that? Showing off Shamrock is no bother."

"It's no bother," Abbi repeated, her eyes innocent, like she didn't know she was getting away with doing exactly what she'd been begging to do.

"I think it's time for a...a nap. You need a nap, Abbi."

"I'm not tired, and you were going to go on a walk without me even though I wanted to see the Blarney Stone. So now you can go on your walk, and I can go with Franny to see the magic stone. Keen!"

"I really don't mind," Franny insisted. "Don't

worry, I'll give you my phone number so you can contact me in case you want to talk to her."

"I am not going to let her out of my sight with a stranger."

"But your walk," Abbi said. "What about your super-important walk?"

"My walk can wait." I glanced at the room, grabbed Abbi's purple backpack, which mewled, and handed it to her. "Stay, Lorde," I said.

Lorde lifted her head, yawned, and lay back down.

I'd already put water out for her, and she'd done her business, so I knew she'd be fine sleeping in the cool room for however long it took me to drag Abbi away from the stone.

I locked the door. Abbi wrestled into her backpack then took my hand. "Thank you. This is going to be so fun!"

"So fun," I said. Then to Franny, "How far is it?"

"Just a few blocks from here. Are you comfortable walking?"

"Yes."

"In those shoes?"

"Something wrong with my boots?"

"No, but it is hot. We can stop for water, if you want. You look a bit flushed."

"I don't want water."

"Ice cream," Abbi repeated for the millionth time. "That will keep us cold. We can get ice cream. Even if it's not the best, I bet it will be good."

"Wonderful," Franny said. "Follow me."

She started across the parking lot like a woman on a mission.

"This motel has been here since 1959. It's changed names, of course. It used to advertise having the luxury of televisions in powder rooms. There used to be a heated pool, right here in the middle of the parking lot. Why, I don't know how cars didn't end up in the middle of it."

She prattled on, pointing at the horseshoe building behind us, then went on about a water tower and gas station.

"Thank you," Abbi said quietly.

I grunted.

"I'll give you my free scoop. The first one anyway." I knew she was apologizing, or maybe just acknowledging that I was in a mood.

It was hard to think of her as a conniving little deity sometimes, especially when she delighted in being a child most of the time.

But it was easy to remember she was our friend and had wriggled her way into my heart. She meant well. Even when ice cream was on the line.

"I'll let you pick the second scoop," she said, squeezing my hand.

I squeezed hers back. "You'd better."

CHAPTER SEVEN

Somehow, Abbi wheedled her way into getting ice cream before seeing the Blarney Stone.

Oddly, the ice cream was found in a restaurant, and it wasn't the same shop as the one listed on the flyer.

The woman who took our order wasn't named Billy. Her name was Stephanie, and she looked like a bored high-schooler.

Because she was a bored high-schooler.

Franny chatted her up, explained the sister-town agreement between the two ice cream shops, which, according to her, were owned by the same partners.

Somehow the coupons got involved and by the time it was over, I had a double scoop cone, Abbi had a bowl with three scoops, and Franny had a single scoop.

Franny sat across from Abbi, and I split the difference between them, taking up a lot of space, facing the window.

It wasn't hot in the place, but it wasn't cold enough to keep the ice cream from melting either. We all set to getting the creamy sweets under control, and after a couple bites, I realized I should have gotten a bowl instead of a cone.

I wiped out the top scoop and had the second whittled down low enough it wasn't dripping over my fingers when I tuned back into the conversation.

"Road trip. That sounds exciting." Franny ate her ice cream in half-spoon bites, like she wanted to make it last twice as long.

"It is! We were in Missouri, that's where I'm from, and then we went to Oklahoma and Kansas, well, Kansas and Oklahoma, and now we're here. I want to see all the sights up close. Really close."

Abbi squirmed around and produced the brochure with the information about the Blarney Stone.

"See?" She spread it on the table and pointed. "Someone buried a lot of cars. I want to see that. And that tower is leaning. And there's the Blarney Stone."

"Route 66." Franny reassessed me. "You're taking her on a road trip down Route 66?"

"What's wrong with Route 66?"

"Nothing. I just..." She paused, and the air shifted, almost as if a window had been opened, allowing in a cooler breeze.

It wasn't uncomfortable. But it was most definitely magic.

"So, what, exactly are you, and what, exactly do you want from us?" I licked the edge of the cone and took a bite. I liked to get cone and ice cream in each bite once I got down to this point.

"Do I need to be anything other than what you see?" she asked.

"When someone uses magic," I said, crunching to the cone point, then popping it in my mouth, "it's pretty hard to ignore."

Her eyebrows arched, and her eyes, a pretty hazel threaded with brown, locked onto me.

"You really should come to the bar," she said.

I wiped sticky fingers on a napkin, which did more clinging than cleaning. "The bar in town? Which one?"

"No, not here. It's up a-ways."

"On the Route?"

"Yes. A small town. Have you heard of McLean?"

"Sure."

"Oh, so you've driven this way before?"

"Sure."

"Maybe I should ask you what *you* are, Brogan Gauge."

There was that breeze again, coming in through a window that didn't exist, brushing over my skin like silk. It smelled like shade and creek water, loamy and sweet.

"I'm exactly what I look like," I said.

She brightened. "Oh, good. So am I."

Abbi tipped her bowl and slurped the melted slurry. "Why do you want him to go to the bar?"

"The same reason I wanted to take you to the best ice cream there. I think he'd like it."

"No. You want him to see something, I think," Abbi said. "Plus, you think you know me."

"You seem...familiar."

"I know."

Franny stared at her bowl a moment as if making a decision. She scraped up the last half spoon of ice cream, then placed her spoon in the bowl.

"Let's see the Blarney Stone. I will tell you more then." She scooted her chair back and stood.

"Yes!" Abbi bounded out of her chair. "It's okay," she said, taking Franny's hand, and tugging her to the door. "He's not mad at you. He knows you're using magic. So do I. You should just tell us why."

Franny threw me a look. I raised my eyebrows, agreeing with Abbi. Before Franny could speak, Abbi pushed through the door.

"What happens if someone licks the stone?" Abbi asked. "Is that good luck or bad luck? Is it extra luck because it gets in your stomach? Can you swallow luck? What does it taste like? Brogan, I bet it's delicious!"

"Abbi," I said, following them into the heat.

Abbi hopped on one foot, then the other, pausing to check for traffic before releasing Franny's hand and bouncing across the street. "Is it this way? I think it's this way. You look like I'm right. Of course I'm right. I'm always right! I'm so excited! How big is it? It must be huge! The biggest, luckiest stone ever!"

"Abbi," I picked up my pace. "Don't run." There was no traffic, but I didn't want her getting lost.

"It's right over there!" She pointed at the archway

on the corner with a little courtyard beyond. Then she ran.

"That's it!" Franny called out. She put on some steam and pulled ahead of me. "Abbi, Abbi, dearest. Wait up. I can tell you all about it."

Abbi didn't need me protecting her from Franny. But I was in a bad mood, and letting Abbi out of my sight with a stranger reminded me too much of Lu and the monster hunter.

"Hey." A hand around my left wrist pulled violently enough, I stumbled mid-pivot like a whipcrack in a kids' game.

I cocked my right fist, but the asshole who had grabbed my wrist twisted. My knuckles hit shoulder, instead of the guy's jaw.

He grunted from the impact. But instead of staggering away, he moved up into my space, into my reach, and simultaneously lifted my left arm and hand, then pressed my hand backward with one swift, incredibly powerful motion.

The bone popped, and I yelled.

The guy was fast—vampire fast—darting around and behind me, his hand over my mouth, arm across my neck.

"Shit," he said. "Shit. I didn't want..."

I was burning under the waves of pain. I could feel the tension in his body, smell the sweat. I raised my boot to stomp on his foot.

"Brogan! The luck!" Abbi yelled. For someone so small, she had a set of lungs on her.

The vampire released and pushed me all in one

motion. I spun toward him, but he was already four yards away and running.

Cowboy. I got the impression of worn jeans, boots, a tucked-in western-style shirt. His hair was brown, clean cut. Good-enough-looking guy made greater from the glamor of the vampiric kind.

Just before he disappeared around the block, he held up his hands—in what? Surrender? Apology?

I wanted to kick the shit out of him.

But between one blink and the next, he was gone.

Fucking vampires are too fucking fast.

My heart thundered, my breath dragged ragged and hard.

Abbi!

I tucked my broken wrist against my chest and ran out of the space between buildings where he'd dragged me.

Electric shocks jolted up my arm with each step, lightning searing stitches through my shoulder, my spine, my skull. Every breath hurt.

I ran harder.

"Abbi!" I rounded the corner and barreled into the little space fenced in on three sides with a concrete pedestal in the center.

Abbi stood on her tiptoes, her palms spread on the top of the pedestal. Franny was beside her, hand under her arm to help stabilize the girl.

"I haven't licked it yet," Abbi said, "so I don't have luck, but Franny told me all about it. Did you know the one in Ireland is bigger than this one because it's the mommy stone and this is only a wee baby stone?"

"Abbi," I breathed, relieved she was still here, still whole, unhurt, babbling and bouncing from too much sugar.

"I wanted to wait so you could see..." She let go of the pedestal.

"You hurt your hand." She rushed to me, touching my elbow. "Did you fall?" Then her eyes went wider. "You got hurt."

"It's fine," I said. "Just a sprain. We have a wrap back in the motel. Lick the stone, Abbi. I think we need that luck."

"I know what did that," she whispered.

I didn't doubt she could tell I'd been jumped by a vampire.

A cowboy vampire who had broken my wrist and run off like he'd stepped into the wrong room filled with garlic, sunlight, and wooden stakes.

It didn't make sense. Things that wanted to hurt, hurt. And vampires were always things that wanted to hurt.

"Are you all right?" Franny asked. "You're pale as a sheet."

"It's fine, I'm fine."

"That wrist?" The feathers in her hair lifted in the breeze. "Mr. Gauge. I know a very good general practitioner who could see you."

"No. I'm fine. Kiss the stone. It's okay, Abbi. Lick it." I pushed her gently toward it with my good hand.

I was sweating, but shivered at every shift in the wind. Shock.

"You need to kiss it too," Abbi said. "You need luck. And a wish. Franny said wishing is allowed because it's magic." She held onto my good elbow and guided me over to the pedestal.

The relief of seeing her unharmed made me too tired to resist. "You need luck for you and Lula," she said. "And maybe you need a doctor too."

"I don't need—"

"Luck, first."

I quickly scanned the engraving on the polished top of the pedestal, where a plaque containing the slice of the stone was displayed.

"You do it first," Abbi said. Hado was on her shoulder, a shadow half-hidden in her hair, with glinting eyes and sharp claws.

I placed the fingertips of my good hand on the side of the plaque.

Luck was automatic, given for the price of a kiss, but wishing was something I'd lost the knack for years ago.

Wishes weren't the same as deals with gods. They didn't have loopholes or prices. Until they were granted. And those loopholes and prices changed depending on who was doing the granting.

I had no idea what a stone might demand. Big wish or little? Big price or small?

I formed the idea. Then I kissed the stone, taking what luck it would give, and repeated the wish once, twice, three times.

"My turn!" Abbi tippy-toed again, smooched (licked) the stone noisily, then mouthed her wish.

If my lip-reading skills were any good, it had something to do with cookies.

"That's it," I said. "Let's get back to the motel. Franny, this is where we part ways."

"Are you sure you don't need help wrapping your wrist?"

"I do not. Let's go now, Abbi."

Abbi had crouched down and was staring at little pebbles at the base of the pedestal. She popped back up and took my hand.

"Don't forget to come see us at the bar," Franny said. "Free appetizer and, of course, the ice cream. Did I mention the ice cream?"

We were walking toward the hotel, but her voice wasn't getting any fainter.

"She's following us, isn't she?" I asked Abbi.

"She likes me."

"You?"

"I like her too."

I sighed.

"She gave me three scoops of ice cream. Three. You only ever let me have two." Her voice was petulant, but she squeezed my arm. She was worried. Probably worried about me.

I was worried too. Not about my wrist. There was a vampire in town, one who broke my wrist then ran off, and I didn't know where Lula was.

I glanced behind me. Franny spotted my glare and

suddenly became interested in a brambly old rose growing on the corner of a fence.

We walked a little faster.

"Vampire, Abbi."

"I know."

"Did you see him?"

"No. I was looking for luck." She paused. "It isn't easy to scry when something is stuck in concrete."

"Scry?"

"I can *see* things. You know I can. I just have to see them at the right, um...angle? Light? And the Blarney Stone is luck. That's a kind of magic. I wanted to see. See if we end up okay."

She leaned into me a little, then must have remembered my injury and quickly pulled away. "Do you think we are?" she asked. "Okay?"

There was a vampire in the town. The woman behind us had some kind of magic up her sleeve and wouldn't leave us alone.

Lula was talking to a hunter who wanted us dead, and two gods—well, a god and a demon, which made it worse, really—had decided they wanted a slice of our current shit pie.

Abbi knew all that. That wasn't what she wanted from me. I knew what she needed. I needed it too.

"Yes," I said. "We are going to end up okay. I promise."

She was quiet for the next block or so. I glanced over my shoulder again.

Franny leaned back giving the roof of the hardware store a good once over.

"I think I want to see the ocean again," Abbi said. "It's been a long time."

"We can do that."

"Ordinary is by the ocean," she said. "Crow lives there."

"Why do you call him Crow?"

"He's only Raven when he's being a god. When he's being a friend, he's funny and smart and just Crow."

"Have you been friends for a long time?"

She smiled. "Yes. He's fun to watch. Did you know he tried to steal a Valkyrie feather once? That didn't work. At all. He almost got killed. But it was funny."

"Do you trust him?" I asked. "If we find the book and take it to Ordinary, do you think it will be safe?"

She hummed. "Ordinary is different. I see some of it. Some of it isn't for me to see, and that's okay." She brightened. "If we go there, I *could* see all of it. Maybe even the magic library!"

We were almost at the motel, the heat simmering up off of the concrete turned my stomach and made my head ache.

"Ordinary is good, though," Abbi said, and it sounded like she was convincing herself along with me. "It's a safe place for all kinds of people. Even people like me."

"Like you?"

"Rabbit in the moon down from the sky. I could… play there. Me and Hado would be safe there."

"Even with all those gods on vacation?"

She nodded. "Sometimes they're better that way."

"Like Crow?" I asked.

"Like Crow."

"What do you know about the demon?"

"He left the Underworld a long time ago." She paused as if gathering up memories. "He caught a lot of souls. He's very good at hiding."

"And catching souls," I said.

"He doesn't do that anymore."

"All demons take souls," I said.

"No," she insisted. "He caught a soul who changed his mind."

"What kind of a soul makes a demon stop taking souls?"

She shrugged. "Just a good man from Ordinary."

"You're really selling this town, kid."

We were at our room now and she hurried to open the door. "I want to see the ocean and the magic library. Maybe…maybe someday we can do both?"

She looked so small and hopeful, I gave her the comfort I could. "Maybe someday we can."

The air that poured out of the room was at least twenty degrees cooler. The pain in my hand and arm was ramping up, and my mind was fixed on setting the damn thing or wrapping or splinting it.

That was my only excuse for not immediately registering that there was a woman in our room.

"Are you hurt?" She was short, maybe an inch under five foot, her gray hair cut in a smart bob. Her glasses were small, wire-rimmed octagons, and her eyes behind them were shrewd.

She wore a light shirt with a long, lighter overshirt that stirred as she moved.

Silk, I thought. It had a way to it, a movement. It had to be silk.

All her colors were green and rose. She looked like a garden.

"You." She pointed to my wrist. "Hurt?" Like maybe I couldn't speak English. She waved at an old-fashioned doctor's bag on the bed.

"You need to sit. I have medicine."

That's when my brain finally caught up to reality. "What are you doing here? Who are you? How did you get into the room?"

"Yes, thank you, he means," Abbi said. "You can help us."

The woman's gaze tracked to Abbi, and something in her body language settled. "I didn't believe her," the woman said, like we were all in on this conversation, except I, for one, had no idea what she was talking about.

"Franny has a way of embellishing things," she said, "but she was right. Hello, moon goddess. I hope you don't mind me not doing the worshiping yet. I'd rather get Brogan patched up first."

CHAPTER EIGHT

Sitting in a hotel room with two women—witches, come to find out—who were doting on a certain little Moon Rabbit, who was secretly an attention-starved starlet, didn't do much for my mood.

That I was the least important person in the room was evident. That Abbi was the most important was also evident, and she was eating it up like a three-scoop bowl of ice cream.

I'd find it funny if I weren't being bossed around.

I'd been instructed to pull up the spare chair and sit, and to hold my arm steady.

"Hold it level," the doctor, Cassia said. "Level, please."

"It is level." I shifted my hand trying to straighten it out. "Enough." The pain throbbed—less if I didn't move it, all the way up to stabbing if I did.

The pills Cassia had given me—

—"*Ibuprofen. Stop looking at it like it's poison. When I want to poison you, I'll put it in your beer or hide it in a cook-*

ie." She regarded me through narrow eyes. "Or a chunk of cheese."—

—did some good to take the edge off.

"It's fractured," she said, while digging in the doctor's bag on the bed next to her.

"Might be broken, but—" She looked up at me. "Wiggle your fingers."

I wiggled.

"Fractured," she muttered, pawing through the bag again. The clatter of glass and metal and something that sounded a lot like a startled frog filled the air. "Let's start here."

She withdrew a modern brace, an Ace bandage, cotton, cotton pads, and a small brown bottle of liquid. One last swipe through the bag produced a soft towel, which she spread over my lap.

"How long have you been on the road?" Her voice was slightly kinder now that she'd settled into applying first aid. She spread a matching towel on the bed and staged the supplies.

"You can't tell?"

"I'm a witch, not a psychic." She nodded to herself. "More than a short lifetime, that much I can see."

"One long lifetime," I said. "Overly long."

"A curse or circumstances?"

"What's the difference?"

"This might hurt. Hold steady. And level." She gave me a pointed look.

I corrected the angle of my arm. The liquid was first, tipped out onto cotton pads. I was taken by how gently she worked, to sanitize my skin, elbow to fingertip.

"A curse has intention behind it," she said in a softer voice. "Someone has to draw it up. Someone has to pay a price to make it viable. To make sure it sticks."

I grunted.

"Many different sorts of people and things can do it. Set a curse." She dropped the used pads into the cheap plastic trash can, then picked up a terry cloth and dabbed at the moisture left on my skin.

I shivered.

"I'm…experienced in spotting curses," she said. "Have a knack, if you understand."

"Sure," I said. "It's one of your specialties because you've had practice cursing a lot of people."

She chuckled, and it was deep and wet. "Let's just say I've spent a few years perfecting my interests."

"Cursing people," I repeated.

"Well, not just people," she allowed. "I'm not speciesist."

She discarded the cloth and picked up a roll of fluffy cotton with a stitched backing. "Lift."

I lifted. She wrapped the cotton, starting around my knuckles and working her way to mid-forearm.

"You don't think I'm cursed?" I said.

She made an indeterminate sound. "Curses work a certain way, follow certain rules. To undo them takes skill."

"Gods have skills."

She stopped, scissors in one hand, cotton spooled

out in the other. "Are you telling me the Moon Rabbit removed your curse?"

"No."

It was her turn to grunt. "One of the meddling gods then. A trickster?"

When I didn't answer, she snipped the cotton and tucked the end of it into place.

"There are gods I won't get involved with," she said. "There are gods you shouldn't get involved with, either."

"Who said I was involved?"

She drew thin, stretchy bandaging off a roll and repeated the wrapping process.

"I think…I'm aware our meeting isn't a coincidence, Mr. Gauge. I've been surrounded by magic since my first breath. I can recognize when the Fates are poking their fingers in my eyes."

She finished with the wrap, then picked up the arm brace, tugging on the tabs. Hook and latch scratched apart in short, quick jerks.

"We—my family—have fallen into difficulties." She nodded toward Franny who was listening in rapt awe to Abbi telling a story about werewolf ghosts and moon cookies. "Choices and actions we've made. Things that aren't easily undone."

She carefully positioned the brace on my arm and indicated I could let go of my wrist. She took over, placing the brace and supporting my wrist before letting me put my hand back under it.

She threaded tabs through slots, pulling the brace tight.

"I was searching for our answer, and here you are now. I think you're our answer, Brogan Gauge. Or at least part of it. But before I can ask you the questions, I need to know which gods you're tangled with."

She pressed the last straps across my palm, her fingers warm and firm.

"Wiggle," she ordered.

I wiggled my fingers.

She squeezed each of my fingertips, looked at my nails, then sat back and folded the towel in her lap. "Let go of your wrist. Let's see how it feels."

I released my wrist, ready for the pain, but it was muffled. "It's good," I said. "Doesn't hurt as much."

"It will as the swelling goes down. Tighten the straps if it feels too loose, but don't tighten it so much you lose circulation in your fingers. Understand?"

"Not my first fracture."

"Good. Then I'll spare you the lecture on what to do if you run a fever, if you become nauseous, if you feel dizzy."

"Rest, elevate, hydrate," I recited.

"Someone's taught you well." She braced her palms on her thighs, elbows sticking out to the side, reminding me, fleetingly, of a grasshopper ready to jump.

"Gods," she said. "How many are you connected to?"

"Questions like that usually come with prices to be paid."

"All right, here's my ante. I'm a witch, you know that. I'm part of a powerful coven. We have connections. Connections that will help you with your vampire problem," she pointed at my wrist, "your past curse problem, and if you play your cards right, your finding whatever it is you're searching for problem—yes, I can see that in you too.

"We—my family—can help you find the thing you're tied to. The thing you can't figure how to cut free of."

The spellbook, of course.

She nodded. "Whatever just put that look on your face? That's the thing we can find."

"How can you find something when you don't even know what it is?"

"Because I'm a witch, not a whiner. So. Tell me which gods have you dancing on their strings? I'll tell you what I want you to do for us, and we'll find the thing…it's magic, isn't it?" Her nose went up like she had caught the scent of something on the wind. "You're looking for something made of god magic."

"I didn't say–"

"You didn't have to. I'm not a psychic, but I am no fool. Make a decision, Mr. Gauge. Tell me the gods you're connected to in exchange for our assistance, or I'll just move on. I'll even throw in the brace for free."

This was something I wanted to do with Lula. A risk, a decision we should both agree to take.

But I didn't know where she was, and the pain and shock of being attacked by a vampire—

—*Lula blank-eyed on the floor. I couldn't move, was pretty sure I'd stopped breathing. All I could do was watch the monster bend over her and sink its teeth into her neck*—

83

I wiped my face with my good hand, glanced at Abbi who was sitting on the back of the couch braiding Franny's hair. Franny sat on the seat cushion below her watching me.

Lorde hadn't been bothered by the witches in the room, content to snooze on the couch, her head on Franny's lap.

Which, I supposed, was a sign of its own of how dangerous the witches were.

Lula had made decisions without me—had spent a lifetime doing so.

But this time it was up to me.

Abbi had been right. We needed friends, or if not that, allies. And so far, Franny and Cassia had been helpful and not unkind.

It was a risk to trust them. But there wasn't any way to live a life without risk.

"We are tied to one god," I said. "Have only made promises to one—Cupid."

Cassia's eyebrows rose. "One of the old gods. Are there others you've crossed paths with?"

"Death."

She blinked. "*Very* old gods. Is that it?"

I hesitated.

"Who else?"

"We've met Raven."

"Of course he's in the middle of this."

"Not in the middle," I said. "He made an offer. We haven't taken it. Not really."

"An offer from a trickster god? More like a slow stabbing with a dull blade. Anyone else?"

84

"There is a god who has hunted us and tried to kill us. Atë."

She sucked a breath and held it, fingers digging into her thighs. "*There's* the problem."

I grunted.

"Did you cross her?" she asked.

"We weren't the ones who started this. Lifetimes ago, she sent monsters to attack us, to change us."

"Were the monsters vampires?" Cassia said it as if she'd heard this story before, as if she knew my past as well as I did.

"Why would you think that?"

She released her thighs, tipped her head down, and looked up at me. "Because, Brogan Gauge, vampires are the problem we need help with. Not just any vampires, but the ones who I think turned you into a spirit and Lula into *thrawan*."

CHAPTER NINE

The ringing in my ears was louder than the air conditioner.

"How?" It came out as a whisper, too soft for me to hear it. "How do you know?"

"That's a longer story." Cassia stood. "No, I'm not brushing you off. But to explain what we want you to do for us, you'll need to come to the coven."

She reached into her back pocket and offered me a business card.

I took it and stood to stop her from leaving, but I was too slow, too rocked by her casual announcement of knowing the whereabouts of the monsters we'd spent fruitless years searching for.

She patted my shoulder and stepped around me.

"I know it's a shock. But I'll let you think on it. Decide if you want to work with us. If you want us to look for the thing that's lost. I think we might be able to help each other."

She was across the room now. Abbi still sat on the

back of the couch, Hado over her shoulders, her feet brushing the seat cushions.

Franny patted the braids in her hair as she left the room. I hadn't even noticed her move.

"Good-bye, Cassia," Abbi said.

Cassia bowed. "Good-bye, Moon Rabbit. I will add a candle to my altar for you."

Then she left, too, and the door clicked shut behind her.

"That was fun," Abbi said.

"Witches? Fun?" I didn't know why that was the only thing that came out of my mouth.

My brain had stalled. I'd glimpse a light, a truth, a hope too bright for me to comprehend, too stark to believe. Cassia knew where the monsters were hiding.

"They like me," she said.

"They're witches."

"I like witches. You want to go to the coven, don't you? Tonight? I mean we got all that good luck. We should use it before it runs out."

I pulled my hand up to rub my face and noticed the card I was holding.

THE BUCKIN' BRONC HONKY TONK

"It's a bar," I said.

"They have ice cream."

"Bars don't have ice cream."

"But they're witches. They can do what they want."

"Honky tonk witches."

"I bet honky tonk witches have ice cream *and*

cookies," she said. "I have luck! If they don't have it, I can ask them to."

"Ask who?" Lula stood in the doorway, her tigress eyes taking in the room, the medical supplies in the trash, Abbi on the couch, and finally me.

"Lu," I said.

Something close to pain, maybe guilt, flashed like a dove's wing across her face.

She didn't move, hadn't even closed the door on the swampy heat. But her gaze took in my boots— scuffed from the fight and the walk back over here— my trousers, sweaty shirt, and held on the brace wrapping my arm and hand.

"How bad?" she asked as she catalogued the rest of me, neck, chin, mouth, cheeks, nose, and then, finally, *finally*, my eyes.

"A sprain."

"Sprain?" she asked somehow directing it at Abbi.

"The witch says it's a fracture," Abbi supplied.

"Witch." Lula's expression remained flat. She shut the door, pausing to press fingertips against its worn surface before she turned back to me.

"Yup. Witches," Abbi said. "We got luck *and* ice cream. You missed both of them, Lula. You missed a lot."

That statement didn't sound much like a young girl had said it. It sounded like an older being who had stared down at the world for time on end and had seen life spool out beneath her. Who had watched millions of people spend their handful of days looking away, walking away, ignoring the very heartbeat that anchored them to time, to the world, and to those who mattered to them.

Or maybe that was just me still in shock.

Lula gestured for me to sit on the bed. I did. Lu took my place in the chair, and then leaned forward, her fingertips touching my brace.

"What did I miss?"

Who hurt you? That was what she was really asking. Who had done enough damage that I had broken.

Stubbornness rose up and closed my throat. I didn't want to tell her. *Fragile.* The accusation still stung.

"Abbi's right," I said. "We got ice cream."

Her slow blink was the only sign of her annoyance. "Abbi?" she asked.

"He only got two, but I got three scoops. You're mad at him or mad at yourself, so I don't want to talk about ice cream. Ice cream is too *good* to be mad about."

"I'm not mad," she said.

"Not about ice cream," I added.

Lu gently touched the back of my fingers. "Not about ice cream."

"You need luck," Abbi said. "You need to kiss the Blarney Stone."

"Maybe I already did."

"No," Abbi said, serious again. "You didn't."

"Have you been spying on me, Abbi?" Lula asked without looking away from me.

"You're easy to see. Both of you are easy to see."

I wasn't sure if that was a yes or a no.

"How did you fracture your arm?" Lu finally asked.

"A fight."

Yes, I was being stubborn. Because anyone could get hurt in a fight—

—*fragile*—

—even she could get hurt in a fight. She had been hurt, more than once, most recently at the hands of Atë. That didn't make either of us fragile.

She squared her shoulders. It took several breaths of us staring at each other before some of that hardness eased.

"Who did you fight?" she asked.

"Didn't get his name. It's nothing, Lu. I'm fine."

She leaned back, taking her soft touch with her and leaving an ache in me.

If I told her I'd been jumped by a vampire, it would explain the fracture. Hell, she might be relieved that all I had ended up with was a bum wrist.

Or she might use my newest failure as another reason to close herself off, to walk away. To leave me and fight our battles without me.

"Where were you?" I asked.

"Walking."

"Did you find him?"

Her gaze cut to mine, startled.

"I know you were looking for the hunter. To clean up the mess I made of it earlier, right?"

"This isn't something you need to be a part of."

"Finding Hatcher?" I asked. "Or hearing the deal you made with him?"

She was a coiled spring, a snake drawn back before the strike. She wanted to deny my assumptions, my accusations. Instead, she folded her arms and stared at the medical trash in the can.

"Yes, I found Hatcher." She looked back at me, arms still defensive. "I didn't make a deal with him. He says he has information. He says he knows where we can find the book. But he wants something in return for the information and won't tell me what it is."

My breath went shallow as I processed that. She'd met with the hunter without me—

—*fragile*—

—and all he could offer was the same false promise we'd heard from god, demon, and witch.

"You could have been hurt," I said. "*Are* you hurt?"

"He didn't touch me, Brogan. I wouldn't let him hurt me. I don't think he could if he tried."

"Because you're stronger than any man? Stronger than me?"

"No. Because I wouldn't let him get near me, of course."

I raised my eyebrows, and color flushed across her pale skin.

"This time. I didn't let him near me this time." She hesitated, then said, "I don't think he's human."

"Great. That's what we need. Another supernatural tied up in all this. What do you think he is? God?"

She shook her head, and her arms loosened. "He

passes as human but isn't a god. We'd both know if he were a god."

"Like we knew Mad Mat was a god?"

"Fair," she said. "We really failed spotting that, didn't we? Mad Mat."

The *we* got me. I smiled. A little crooked, a little wry, but a smile. "We were young and innocent."

Her body relaxed as she sat back against the chair. "We were stupid."

"Sure," I said. "That too. Which is to be expected from a couple kids. We've learned a lot. We've been through a lot."

She glanced at my arm, then back to me.

"Both of us have been through a lot," I said, trying to find the words to tell her I understood her fear for me, because I carried the same fear for her.

I searched for the words that would bring her back to me or bring me to her. I wanted to be inside the walls she'd put up for my safety, for her own.

We were better together, our strengths and weaknesses balancing and bracing.

"I'm sorry." I lifted my wrapped arm. "For this."

She shook her head, but I went on. "I'm sorry you…sorry Atë…the farmhouse. You were hurt, I know you were hurt, and I wish I could have…."

"Brogan, don't…it's…that isn't... I'm fine. Fine about that."

"But we're not fine, love. I want to fix us. Fix me, if that's the problem."

She touched my arm.

I was breathing hard, working against a tidal wave of emotions.

"We could walk away," I blurted.

She blinked. "From what?"

The air felt heavier, hotter. The air conditioner chugged, its cold breeze stabbing stiff, ineffective fingers into the space.

Abbi whispered nonsense words to Lorde, who was making noises back at her. Maybe she had her own language. Maybe the Moon Rabbit spoke Earth Dog.

"From everything," I said catching at my drowning thoughts.

This. This was the one thing I'd never allowed myself to consider all these years.

That maybe it hadn't been love holding us together, but that the reason we'd stayed with each other, held hope for each other, was only so we could get revenge on the monsters that had destroyed our lives.

"The Route." I cleared my throat. "The search for the spellbook. The search for the monsters who attacked us. Everything. We could walk away from everything."

Had I said too much? Asked too much of her?

"Is that what you want?" Her voice was carefully neutral. No teasing lilt, no sardonic eyebrow rise.

"I want us," I said.

She licked her bottom lip. "This *is* us, Brogan. It has always been us."

"Our life has always been chasing something out

of our past? Chasing things that hurt us or that other people want us to find for them? When we were alive…"

"That life is gone."

"We can…"

"No. We can not," she said very clearly. "We aren't innocent. We aren't children. Not anymore. Not for years." She glanced away again, her gaze falling to the medical trash.

"I…I am trying to appreciate your intent," she said, as if she were feeling out a cliff's edge. "You want to…take a break from…*this*."

"That's not…"

"You haven't lived as long as I have," she said, "in flesh. I can't speak for your experience as a spirit, but this way," she spread her hands, opening her body language to indicate herself, her flesh, her bones, the life she'd been forced to live, alone, lonely, "isn't easy."

Her eyes were the gold of summer, of riches. The gold of dreams. They held a distance I'd never seen before.

"That isn't." I inhaled and shivered, pushing emotion away. "Okay. Let me try again. Ever since we agreed to Cupid's deal, we've been pulled deeper into conflicts with gods. We've been hurt—both of us have been hurt. I don't like that. I don't want that."

Her nod was short, almost imperceptible.

"I'm just asking, are we still okay doing what we're doing—making deals with the gods and demons. I am just asking if hunting the monsters who attacked us and took away a hundred years of us being together, is how we want to live the life we have, the days and years we have left.

"If it is," I said, "then that's what we'll do. I will be beside you, love, every step of the way. But if you want to solve this on your own—meet Hatcher who wants you dead—without me at your side, and if I'm going to be attacked by vampires without you at my side," her fury at the mention of vampires was stark, but I bullishly continued, "then we need to reassess how we're going forward, how we're living."

"Vampire?" she asked.

"Yes. Earlier today."

"After ice cream," Abbi added, proving she'd been paying attention. "Before the luck, though," she said, "because a vampire attack isn't lucky. Oh. But maybe it is. The witches said they can help us, and they like me, so maybe it is lucky."

Lu was staring at me, but I knew she didn't see me. Whatever was going on in her mind was deep, closed off. I was good at reading her, had spent a lifetime reading her moods, but the woman in front of me could have been a stranger.

I worked on my breathing. Keeping it easy. Steady.

"Witches," she said, gaze snapping into focus as she came back from that distant place.

"Two," I said. "One brought a flyer for a local bar and ice cream coupons. The other was waiting in our room to patch me up."

"What do they want?"

"To make friends with me!" Abbi said.

I hummed. "Maybe that. And, you'll be surprised to hear this, they want to give us what we're looking for if we give them something."

Lu pressed her thumb to her temple as if a headache were building there. "The book?"

"The book. They said they don't know what we're looking for, but they can still find it. They want something from us in return."

"What do they want?" she asked.

"Would it be so impossible to walk away from this?" I asked. "Drive somewhere. Anywhere but here?"

"Brogan," she said softly. "Just tell me. What do the witches want from us?"

Running away from our past wouldn't change our past, and it wouldn't change who we had become. I knew that. It had been a foolish hope.

"They want our help with a vampire." I cleared my throat. "Who they think is the vampire who attacked us all those years ago."

Lula's pupils went wide, a hunter scenting prey. Nothing else about her changed, but I could feel it, her hunger for blood, her hunger for violence. For revenge.

She stood. "Let's go make a deal with the witches."

CHAPTER TEN

A bbi insisted we all take a nap, even Lula, since the bar wouldn't be open for a few hours.

I hadn't thought anyone could make Lula sleep, but Lu agreed to lie down beside me on the lumpy bed. She'd fallen asleep almost immediately. I suspected Moon Rabbit magic was involved, but didn't ask.

Lu hadn't been sleeping much or well. Neither had I.

I pushed at the pillow under my head, then dropped it beside me so I could prop my injured arm on it.

Lula lay curled on her side facing away from me. I placed my good hand on her hip and stared at the ceiling, shivering, but too hot to get under the blanket.

I blinked.

The room was darker, drenched in shadow, bars of late afternoon sunlight seeping through the curtains.

The pillow was still under my elbow. I hadn't moved an inch.

Lula was gone.

Had she left me behind again? Was she making deals with the witches? Hunting the vampire of our nightmares without me?

Fragile.

I rubbed my hand over my face and wished I believed in a god enough to send up a prayer.

"It's okay," Abbi said. "She's still here."

The sound of running water came to me, and I rolled my head to stare at the closed bathroom door.

"Reading my mind?" I asked Abbi.

"You have loud worries."

I rolled my head the other way. Abbi sat on the floor next to Lorde, petting the dog's head.

"You have big ears," I said.

She grinned. "I do. You should see them sometime."

"I'd like that."

Her hand paused in Lorde's thick black fur. "Really?"

"I bet you're a very cute bunny."

She drew herself up. "Rabbit. And yes. I am a *very* cute rabbit. And powerful."

Hado, still a little black kitten, launched out from between the couch pillows, landing squarely on top of Abbi's head.

"Help!" Abbi half-yelled, half-laughed. "I'm being attacked. Help!"

Lorde jumped to her feet, barking at them.

Abbi dissolved onto the ground giggling hard enough to snort, while Lorde licked her face. Hado growled at Lorde with the volume of a much larger creature.

I sat and watched them, bemused. Lula walked up beside the bed and paused, as if unsure if she could touch me.

I took her hand but didn't look away from the wrestling-giggling-barking match.

"Remind me to buy a camera," I said.

"You have one," she said.

"I don't think so."

"You do. Your phone. Where is it?"

I nodded at the bedside table.

She stretched over me, and I caught the scent of her perfume mixed with the overly sharp smell of the hotel bar soap she must have used.

She frowned at the phone, swiped the screen and tapped it. She caught me watching and smiled.

I loved her. I would always love her. No matter how we lived our lives, no matter the choices we made, no matter what our futures might be.

She leaned into me, turning the phone around so I could see the screen. She pointed the device toward the chaos near the couch.

Abbi snickered against the cheap carpet. Hado was perched on top of Lorde's back batting her ears, which made Lorde bark and spin, tail wagging.

"Press this circle." Lula's breath was sweetened with mint. "It will take a picture. You can press it more than once."

Since I was down a hand, she held the phone for me. I did as she said, the phone making a soft *snick*ing sound, imitating a camera click.

"Where does the photo come out?" I asked.

She raised an eyebrow because I may not have used modern technology much, but that didn't mean I hadn't observed her using it over the years.

"Here's the gallery." She tapped and thumbed and there it was. The gallery contained two photos, tiny copies of the menagerie across the room.

It was a wonderful reminder of what technology could do, but I was struck by a wave of sorrow. All these years, and I didn't have a single picture of Lula.

I took the phone and fumbled my way back to the camera. I turned it and while Lu watched with a patient expression, I snapped her photo. More than once.

"I'm not even wearing anything nice," she said.

She was wrong, of course. In the dark green tank top and jeans, with her red hair pulled into a braid over her shoulder and her pale skin pink and fresh from the shower, she looked like the goddess of summer come to lure mortal souls to an eternity of pleasures.

"You are always beautiful."

"This shirt has a stain, and my jeans are ripped."

"You don't see yourself through my eyes," I said.

She smiled, and it was real and whole. "Here." She took the phone and leaned beside me, holding it at arm's length. The screen now showed the both of us.

I was startled at how pale I was behind my tight, dark beard. Startled to see the bruised circles under my eyes. "Sheesh," I said. "Look at that bed head. I should comb my hair."

Her thumb tapped the circle.

"Your hair is perfect," she said. "Messy. Alive. Just how I like you."

I grinned. "Yeah? You like this?"

She rested her head on my shoulder and took one more picture. "I like this. Us."

And oh, how my heart filled with joy.

Abbi and the beasts had finally settled down, Abbi on her back staring at the ceiling, Lorde resting her big head on Abbi's stomach. Hado curled up by Abbi's face.

"Are we going soon?" Abbi asked.

"We are," I said.

"In a minute," Lula said. "Brogan's going to take a shower first."

"Do I stink?"

"You smell good."

"But?"

"You also smell like witch and vampire."

I grunted. So she'd known, or could have known, exactly where I'd been and who I'd been with the moment she'd walked into the room.

"Might need some help with this," I gestured at the brace.

She lifted her head off my shoulder. "Go on in. I'll get some tape."

She knelt next to our duffles and unzipped the side of hers.

I plucked the plastic bag used for ice out of the ice bucket on the top of the dresser and took it with me into the bathroom.

The room was still warm from her shower, and her perfume—honey and roses— hung sweet in the air. I inhaled, filling my lungs with the scent. Filling my mind with memories of her.

My body—my very flesh and blood body—responded to the sensation of warmth, heat, and the familiar scent of the woman I loved.

I chuckled. We didn't have time for fooling around, no matter how much I liked that idea. Instead, I put my mind to reciting baseball stats to calm my blood.

I turned on the shower spigot, then tugged off my T-shirt. When I turned around, the bathroom door closed.

Lula stood there, her eyes filled with a hunger I hadn't seen in a long time.

"Hey, handsome," she said.

"Hey, yourself."

She held up a roll of duct tape. I pulled the plastic bag out of my back pocket and put it over the brace on my arm.

We both knew there wasn't time for us to linger with each other, to explore.

But we moved a little slower while she sealed the edges of the bag to waterproof my arm. We stood a little closer, breathed each other in, silent in our apologies, gentle in our touches, making promises to each other that we still had time. We were still here, alive, and were more than just two people grieving a past, craving revenge.

There would still be time for us, for our lives, for our future. Because we wanted more than revenge, hardship, and fear. Because we had not given up on hope.

THE NIGHT SKY WAS CLOUDLESS, stars simmering like drops of water on a cast-iron skillet. Bug song filled the air with constant, hard whirring that irritated more than soothed.

We had the windows down, Lula guiding the truck to an empty spot on the concrete and gravel parking lot. Lorde sat at my feet, and Abbi perched between Lula and me.

The tires crunched as Lu slotted Silver into the farthest spot and turned off the engine. Sodium lights burned dust into yellow cones, spotlighting cars, trucks, motorcycles.

The BUCKIN' BRONC HONKY TONK was a flat-topped concrete box that could have been a repair shop before it had gone bar. And while it wasn't big, out here between towns, it was popular enough to half-fill the lot, including a couple 18-wheelers parked in the pullout just down the road.

Neon pentagrams shone in the small dark windows, and the bigger sign across the roof line spelled out its name next to a stylized horse kicking up its back hooves.

Each letter O in the sign had an upside-down five-pointed star in the middle of it.

"Do you smell vampires?" Abbi asked between long sniffs.

"Yes, but I've smelled them since we hit Texas," Lula said. Then to me, "What?"

"You didn't tell me that," I said. "You smell them?"

"I didn't think...I forget, sometimes what it's like to be human."

"I'm not human."

"Closer. You're closer to it than I am."

"I don't think so."

"No, she's right," Abbi said. "You're a lot slower than her. You can't see as good. You can't smell as good. Oh! You can't fight as good either."

Lu pressed her hand over her smile and looked at me over the top of her fingers.

"Thank you so much, Abbi," I said. "That's just what I wanted to hear."

"You're welcome. C'mon! Let's go talk to the witches. They like me." She climbed over my legs, trying to get to the door handle. "I think they're gonna have cookies *and* ice cream!"

"Take it easy," I said, pushing her hair out of my face. "No, don't jerk on the door, let me...just let me...Abbi, don't put your knees..."

"Got it!" she crowed. She pushed, the door swung.

I grunted, trying to protect my wrist and groin as she bolted out of the truck.

"Come on." She jogged toward the building, pausing several feet away from the truck. "Cookies, Brogan!"

"This dessert obsession is going to get you kidnapped and murdered," I muttered.

"I heard that."

"How many?" I asked Lula as I patted the seat next to me, inviting Lorde up onto it so she could stretch out.

"Cookies? I have no idea."

"Vampires."

Abbi was waiting, but she wasn't holding still. She tipped her head back and spun in a circle, watching the stars.

Lu paused, as if trying to hear something beyond the thick chirring of the night. "One. I think."

"In the bar?"

She nodded.

I thought about the gun we'd put in the glove box, but I knew better than to take a weapon that could be turned against me in a fight.

Vampires were fast and strong, and while my dominant hand was fine, my other arm was in a brace. Leaving the gun behind didn't mean I had to go into this empty handed. I got out of the truck.

"Abbi," I asked, coming up next to her. "Can I have one of the gifts?"

She stopped spinning. "The coupons?"

"The feather or the rock."

"Oh, those," she said, relieved. She shrugged out of her backpack and dug around in it. She held the demon rock out to me. "Are you going to call on the demon? With the stone?"

"Not if I can help it." I had no idea what kind of magic the demon stone carried, but there was power in it. Hopefully, it would be something I could tap if we needed it.

Lu brushed her hand across my arm as she walked forward.

Abbi sprang into action and bounded past her. I stayed back with Lorde beside me, watching them, searching the shadows and the fall of light around the vehicles for danger.

Lula moved like a song, fluid and flowing, each part of her shifting in rhythm, the moonlight white of her skin, the fire of her hair, the long, lean lines of her slicing through the night.

It was impossible to look away from her. Impossible not to be caught by her beauty and strength.

And those jeans. There was something about seeing that woman in denim that made my mouth go dry.

She knew it, too, and gave her ass a little extra swing just before she reached the door.

Yes, I smiled.

The music was loud enough—something with a slow country beat—I could hear it through the door.

"I'm going, too," Abbi told Lula. "I'm going," she said to me, as she pointed at the 21 AND OLDER ONLY sign. "I'm not really a little girl. I'm older than any of you, and I want those cookies."

"Bars don't have cookies," I said.

"They will," she insisted. "Because there are witches here and they *love* me." She grinned, showing off her square front teeth, her round face tipped up, eyes absolutely huge.

"Maybe they'll give you carrot sticks, little bunny."

Her eyes somehow got bigger. "Or carrot *cookies*," she breathed. "Go, go." She pushed Lula's hip. "Go in."

Lu cast me a quick question, her eyes glittering like a predator in the darkness. I nodded.

She opened the door, and Lorde slipped up to walk with her, striding into the glow of yellow, green, purple and pink; into the loud, soulful country song—into a room filled with witches.

Just like a scene from a movie, the music abruptly silenced. Every head turned our way.

Lorde *woof*ed softly.

"About time," Cassia called from the bar. "That was very dramatic, Jerry," she said to a man standing behind a sound system on the far side of the empty dance floor. "You can turn the music back on now."

He threw her a salute, and a different song filled the place, this one with a little more twang. I recognized it: "The Redheaded Stranger," sung by John D. Loudermilk.

"You're the redhead," I told Lula. "That makes me the raging black stallion."

She choked back a laugh and cleared her throat.

"Come in," Cassia said. "Have a seat." The witch waved at an open table that would let us keep an eye on the door and most of the room.

Abbi was already halfway across the room, headed straight to Cassia at the bar, elbows out as she held onto her backpack straps, an absolute picture of determination.

"Do you have—"

I gave a soft whistle. Abbi paused and looked back at me. I pointed toward the table. She rolled her eyes but stomped that way. "Cookies?" she yelled over to Cassia.

Half a dozen people stood up. Cassia pointed to a woman with pixie-short hair who looked way too young to be in a bar.

"Go ahead, Pru. Just bring a variety."

Pru sprinted to the door. "I'll be back in a second," she said breathlessly. "Hang on."

Okay, that was weird.

"Cookies are on the way, Moon Rabbit," Cassia said. "Now. You two." She pointed at Lula and me. "Sit. I'll be with you in a moment."

Lula looked like she was going to argue, but I caught her elbow and guided her to the table where Abbi had already claimed a chair.

"They're bringing me cookies," she said triumphantly. "You heard that right? Cookies."

"We heard," Lula said.

"Everyone heard." I positioned a chair so I could watch the bar. Lula sat opposite, her eyes on the door.

"All right everyone," Cassia said to the room at large, "let us begin."

I tensed. Lula tensed. Abbi sat up straighter and stopped swinging her feet.

Everyone in the room—maybe forty people in all —lined up on the dance floor, five lines, seven people long.

"What's happening?" Abbi whispered.

I glanced at Cassia. She sashayed out from behind the bar, plunked a pink cowboy hat on her head, and centered herself in front of the people.

"Hit it, Jerry!"

"Oh," Abbi said, as the slow mellow tones of bass and sweetly pitched steel guitar filled the room. "I like this song."

The people on the dance floor seemed to like it too. It was "Neon Moon," sung by Carrie Under-wood. I'd heard it on the radio more than once while driving the long, lonely Route.

The line dance was intricate and hypnotic, an easy roll and swing, each person separate but joined, linked in those steps, that movement, that song.

They sang along to it, too—not everyone, but most of them—humming, harmonizing, riffing on the melody, and making it something more. Something magic.

It was beautiful. I couldn't look away, didn't want to miss a single move as I tapped my thumb against the table.

Lula had lost the hardness in her body language

and was swaying to the soft vocals, a rapt expression on her face.

Even Lorde was sprawled on the floor, eyes closed, sleeping happily.

Why was she so relaxed? Why was I? *Witches*, a part of my mind reminded me. We'd walked right into a coven of honky tonk witches.

They were dancing. Singing.

They were casting a spell, springing a trap we'd walked right into.

CHAPTER ELEVEN

The room faded, walls fell away. We were surrounded by massive, ancient trees. The moon—not neon but full and white and pure—shone down around us, lighting the forest, the grasses we sat upon, the arc and jut of leaf and branch.

Flower petals tumbled from the star-speckled sky —roses, mountain laurel, blue bonnet, sage— blending with the scent of juniper pine on the air, creating a heady perfume.

It was a spell. It was more.

Sorrow, hope, a plea.

The song lyrics spoke of missing a lover, but the spell spoke of missing the moon, missing the full pure light—and of missing family, home, life.

They had lost someone.

That realization hit hard, and I knew it was true. They had lost someone they loved, and now they were bearing witness, promising worship, and asking for blessing and guidance as they tried to right this terrible wrong.

This dance, this spell wasn't about trapping us. It wasn't about me and Lu at all.

It was for Abbi. It was for the moon deity.

Abbi was there, somehow now in the center of their dance, perched on a small hill, the dancers circling around her.

She was still the Abbi I knew—a young girl with the huge eyes and a round face—leaning so far forward over her knees and watching them all so intently, it seemed she'd topple.

But she was more than just a girl. She was a rabbit, strong and lean, both midnight and moonlight, her long ears lifted and turning, her eyes jade green.

Hado was there too, a shadow in man shape, a shadow in cat shape, a shadow in rabbit shape, toad shape, guarding, watching.

As the dance went on, I caught glimpses of another child, a ghostly image, maybe four or five years old, being guided gently from dancer to dancer.

The child was a phantom, a memory of a girl, pale, dark haired, expressionless. Her eyes, when the moonlight touched them, were blood red.

As the song came to an end, silver tears tracked down Abbi's cheeks.

The witches sank down to their knees, hands lifted toward Abbi. In their hands were flowers, leaves, stones, fruits, and yes, cookies.

Abbi stood. The forest was—impossibly—still a forest. Silent.

Light surrounded her, a soft, green power that grew.

In that light she was rabbit, swift and strong and *magic*. "I understand," Abbi said. "I'll do what I can. I promise you we all will."

Lula sighed. "Shit."

I shook my head, but didn't speak. Lu reached for me, found my right hand. I squeezed. Whatever Abbi had just promised us into, we would do it together.

"Now," Abbi said, "let us be where we are."

The forest dropped away. The sky, the night, the soft wind, gone.

I shifted on the hard chair at the table, leaned back, and crossed my arms over my chest, wincing as I forgot my injured left wrist.

Abbi was still out on the dance floor, because of course she was.

The witches—men, women, and others—gathered closer around her, each taking a moment to touch her outstretched hands, leaving the gifts of flowers, leaves, fruit, and cookies in a basket at her feet.

Then they calmly returned to their seats, chatting as if they'd just had a nice lunch social.

Cassia bent and picked up the basket.

Abbi spun toward me and Lula. "We should help them."

I raised my eyebrows.

"Why?" Lula asked.

"I don't think…" Cassia said.

"Just listen," Abbi said, catching Cassia by the

wrist and tugging her to our table. "I know you'll want to help. It's about a little girl."

Abbi pulled chairs out for both of them and waited for Cassia to sit before clambering into the other chair. "Now we can all talk about it," Abbi said.

"Why do you need our help? Who is the child?" Lula asked.

"We don't need your help," Cassia said. "This isn't your business."

"You wanted our help back at the motel," I said.

"Well, yes. But that was before the Moon Rabbit offered hers."

"I promised *all* of our help," Abbi said.

I couldn't hold back my sigh.

"Does she not speak for you?" Cassia asked me.

"We're family," I said with a shrug.

Abbi made a happy sound.

"Of course she speaks for us, even," I added, giving Abbi a look, "when we'd prefer she ask us first. You told us you and your people would find the thing we are looking for. Does that still stand?"

Cassia nodded reluctantly.

"You also told us you know the vampire who attacked us years ago," I said.

"No, I was wrong about that."

That was a lie. Lu stilled beside me.

"I would prefer the truth." I held the witch's gaze. I didn't know what she saw in mine, but she broke first.

"I wasn't wrong about it," she said. "I told you that—I lied on purpose—so you would come here. So you would bring the Moon Rabbit here. But I don't want to complicate things. You," she pointed at me, then Lula, "are complicated."

"And you don't think Abbi is?" Lula asked.

"Oh, I'm not," Abbi said. "I mean, I'm not what I look like, but I'm super simple."

Abbi might think she was what she seemed to be —an adventuresome, slightly silly, sugar-loving child —but I'd seen her march alone into battle against an army of Hush and walk away without a scratch.

"Who did you lose?" Lula asked.

Cassia startled but covered it quickly.

"It was in your spell," Lula went on. "Who is the child you lost, and why are you asking Abbi to get her back?"

"That is not your concern."

Abbi touched the back of Cassia's hand.

"You need them, Elder," she said. "You don't think you do, but I can see. It's why you came looking for us. It's why you fixed Brogan's arm. It's why you invited us here."

Jerry put on a new song with a slow beat that reminded me of distant thunderstorms. The other witches chatted and sipped drinks, eating a variety of surprisingly normal bar foods. Most of them turned to sneak glances at our table like we were newlyweds at a reception.

They wanted to join us but, out of respect, were giving us space.

Cassia sat back. After a moment, she waved at the man behind the bar, and he strolled over to the table.

He was slight, but muscular, a single streak of white cutting through his short, dark hair from just above his pierced eyebrow.

"We might as well order," she said. "I know I need a drink. Wine, please, Stratton. Moon Rabbit?"

"Do you have grass soda?"

"I'm afraid we don't," he said.

"That's okay. Do you have something with cherries in it?"

"That, I can do." His gaze flicked to me.

"Beer," I said. "Dark, if you have it."

"We do. And you?" he asked Lula.

"Wine. Whatever red you have."

He nodded. "Would anyone like something to eat?"

"More cookies?" Abbi asked.

He grinned. "Pru should be back in a minute, Your Glory."

"Oh." Abbi smiled wide.

"Anything else?" he asked.

"Water for Lorde," Lula said.

"Lorde?"

"Our shepherd."

That got a short chuckle out of him. "Of course we'll get her some water. Would she like the beef bone I have back there?"

Lorde sat up, her fuzzy ears turning toward him. She whined softly.

"Yes," Lula said. "Thank you."

He turned back toward the bar.

"He called me Glory," Abbi said. "Did you hear

that, Brogan?" She flashed a big smile. "He gave me a name!"

"You have a name," I said. "Several of them."

"Yeah, but I like that one. Abbi Glory." Hado popped out of the backpack in her lap and mewled up at her.

"That's not your name," I said.

"It could be." She settled Hado on her shoulder. "Abbi Glory Gauge," she whispered. She blinked up at me, her expression asking for my permission. Asking to use our last name.

I pursed my lips and leaned toward her as if sharing a secret.

"That *is* a good name," I said. "But right now we need to deal with the promise you made to the witches."

She turned to Cassia. "Tell them about Rhianna."

"This isn't easy," Cassia said. "We've…we've made mistakes, many mistakes. Some because we didn't have the information we needed, and decisions…that were made in the heat of the moment. You have not found us at our best." She grimaced then seemed to gather herself.

"We've lost more than one person. We've lost two of our coven. One is my son, Variance. The other is his daughter, Rhianna."

Lula nodded and I relaxed. This was familiar ground, and we were good at it. We'd searched for the lost before, searched for Abbi, for Hado. It was part of the deal we'd struck with Cupid—find the lost people, bring them back to who or where they called home.

But Cupid was not behind this, as far as we could tell. He wasn't a part of this promise or bargain.

Stratton strolled over, handed out our drinks, then placed a bowl of water and a bone with meat on it on the floor for Lorde. He patted her head and made himself scarce.

I tried the beer. Cold, hoppy, and bitter in all the right ways.

"Do you know why Route 66 is so special?" Cassia asked. "It isn't just because it helped build a growing country. It's been a way that people, and many other things, have traveled. To explore, expand. To find home. Magical things have always moved along the Route," she said. "Monsters too."

"Like vampires," Lula filled in.

Cassia lifted her wine glass in both a toast and an acknowledgment that Lula had gotten it right.

"They've settled here. A lot of vampires. But we've settled here too. We've found a way to live in… well, not in peace, but not at war. They stay out of our town and territory, and we stay out of theirs. It's been that way for nearly a hundred years."

"But now?" Lula asked. She hadn't touched her wine. She just turned it slowly by the stem, never once looking at it.

"The leader of the vampires—Dominick—has always been vile. He was turned vampire by something powerfully malevolent. He carries darkness that unbalances the flow of the universe. A darkness we have combated and held off for decades.

"One of us, Variance," she added, "made a mistake. He was fool-hearted. He thought he could confront Dominick and force him to ease off of our territory."

She gulped wine, her hand shaking, red staining her pale lips. "He didn't know, couldn't know the consequences of his actions. Couldn't know the horror he would invite into our home."

"Where is he now?" I asked.

"Here," a man said. But it wasn't a man who stepped out of the shadows, it was a vampire.

He looked like he was in his late twenties. His hair was a deep, chestnut brown, his eyes lighter brown, his skin still darkened from a tan that was sure to fade.

He must not have been turned very long ago to still have a tan.

He was also the same vampire who had broken my wrist.

"The hell," I said, fighting the urge to put myself between Lula and him, to grab her and Abbi and run.

"My son," Cassia said. "Variance. Yes, a vampire. Now you know. Do you still want to talk with us? Do you still want to give us aid?" It was a challenge. A dare.

"That's the one who broke my wrist," I told Lula.

"It was a mistake." He held up a hand. "I thought you were stalking Franny and the Moon Rabbit."

Lula hadn't moved, hadn't looked away from

Cassia. "Why is he here if he brought horror into your home?"

"May I sit?" He hadn't taken another step. But I knew how fast he could be. Faster than Lula. Certainly faster than me.

I thought about the stone in my pocket, the one that belonged to the demon. I could draw it out now and take the risk of releasing whatever magic it held.

Lula must have known what I was thinking. She brushed her fingertips on my knee.

"Sit," she said, as much of an invitation as the vampire could expect.

He made a point to move slowly, to move at an exaggeratedly leisurely human speed.

He held my gaze in that unblinking way of vamps.

"I don't like you," I said, just to get it out there.

"Fair. I apologize for breaking your wrist."

I grunted, because I was not used to apologies from monsters.

Only then did he make eye contact with Lula. They were both silent, unbreathing, sizing each other up. Variance was still, his body falling into the razor angles of a predator scenting prey.

No, a predator recognizing danger.

"Variance," he said, in introduction to Lula. "Of the McClellan Coven."

"Lula Gauge," she said like he should have heard of her. And really, he should have heard of her.

"I thought so." He leaned forward, lowering his head in a slow bow. "I've been looking for you, Lula Gauge."

I could feel the surprise in her, the shock at his deference, but Lula didn't move a muscle. "Why?"

"I sent the hunter to find you. To offer you a deal."

Now I officially hated everything about this.

"Unless someone gets to the point," I said, "we're leaving."

Abbi sniffed. "Don't be more mad now. They still need our help."

"I don't give a damn—"

"They lost a little girl," Abbi said. "Are you so mad at vampires and that stupid hunter that you would let a little girl die?"

No. I didn't have that in me. If a child was in danger, I would do what I could to help. I knew Lula was the same.

"Yes," Lula said, and it hit like a punch. "We are that angry at vampires. The child isn't our problem."

That wasn't like her. She'd never turned away from helping an innocent before. I reached for her hand, but it was knotted into a fist.

"You don't mean that," Abbi said. "She doesn't mean that," she told Cassia.

"She's my daughter," Variance went on. "She's been vampire bit."

Lula made a sound, and I squeezed her wrist.

"Did you bite her?" Lu's voice was level, but I could hear the anger there, the horror that a child had endured such an attack.

"No," he said. "Dominick."

"We can save her," Cassia said. "We think it isn't

too late to save her. We can return her to a human, mortal life if we find her soon. We will do that even if you refuse to help us."

"How did this happen?" I asked, horrified. "How does a child pay for her father's mistakes?"

"He called her," Variance snarled. "She…she could not…" The words dried up and his eyes flooded red.

"He was angry," Cassia said. "Furious that Variance had challenged him. We didn't know he had captured Variance. Didn't know until Rhianna slipped away to him, answering a call we could not block. Then. Could not block then. We didn't know how strong Dominick had become. What he could do from his throne." She lifted her glass and took another sip. "We are all at fault."

"Did Dominick come here?" Lula asked.

Cassia shook her head. "Never him. His lackeys have tried to break through our magic, our boundaries. At first, we were not up to the challenge."

"Six people died," Variance said.

"Yes," Cassia snapped. There was a pause, a silence between them. "We have grieved."

"It's not enough," Variance growled.

"We will continue to grieve," Cassia said, her voice rising. "But we must go forward while Rhianna still has time."

"You want revenge?" I asked the vampire.

"I want justice," he countered.

"By us killing Dominick?" Lula asked.

"No." He turned to her, and his smile was deadly.

"I will kill that horror. But before I do, I need your help stealing something from him."

"Is it the book?" Abbi asked.

He shook his head, gaze locked on Lula. "It's my daughter, Rhianna."

CHAPTER TWELVE

"The vampire has your daughter?" I asked.

Cassia pulled off her glasses and sat back. The circles under her eyes were dark, and her shoulders slumped. "She's been gone for two days. We've… we've tried many things to find her. Now, with the blessings of the Moon Rabbit, we will bring her home. We still have time." That last was said in a whisper.

"And you think she's only been bitten once?" Lula asked.

"Yes," Variance said.

Lu's judgmental silence told me just how much she believed that.

"We can heal her and nullify the vampire bite," Cassia said. "But we'll need Dominick's blood."

"Magical healing, for vampire bites. Why haven't I heard of that?" Lu said, locked in a staring contest with Variance.

"You aren't a part of the coven," he replied.

"What about Variance?" Abbi said. "Shouldn't Variance get healed too?"

He jerked and his eyes flooded deep red again.

"No," Lula said. "He's beyond magical healing. Even with Dominick's blood. Aren't you?"

"They held me for three months," he said in an implacable tone. "There is no return for me."

"You want us to get his blood," Lula said.

"I want him dead."

"We want Rhianna home," Cassia cut in. "No one kills him until we have her back. You understand that, Variance. That is the only way to save your daughter. We bring Rhianna home and heal her. That is how you save her. That is what matters."

He didn't respond, still caught in the staring contest.

"What is our part in this?" I asked. "What is our payment?"

"You help us get Rhianna home," Cassia said. "You help us get Dominick's blood. We know who has the spellbook of the gods. We know who has hidden it."

It wasn't that easy. Nothing about that damn book was this easy.

"That is our offer," she said. "We can tell you where the book is and how to retrieve it. In exchange, you will help us save our child."

Easy enough terms for me to agree to. Hell, I'd rescue the girl even if we weren't being paid. But Lula? Lula had been restless lately. Making deals without me. Pulling away and following her own compass.

It bothered me. No, it scared the crap out of me.

If Lula couldn't see the human side of this, if the need for revenge caught her by the throat, and she followed the urge to kill Dominick, or hell, Variance—there would be no reasoning with her, no bargaining.

There would be nothing I could do to stop her.

Lu hadn't immediately gone on the attack, hadn't drawn a weapon on Variance.

She was still talking, which meant she could rein in the urge to kill. That was something.

"The full moon is tomorrow," Cassia said. "We will need your answer by then. If you cannot agree to our terms, then we will do this without you."

There was a shift in the air. Nothing I could put my thumb on, but I knew every witch in the bar was ready to call upon magic to protect, fight, or run.

We were in their territory. No matter how welcoming they had been, this was not our place of power.

"Your terms are…difficult," Lula said.

"I agree," Variance said.

"Good," Cassia said.

"I agree that the terms are difficult," Variance clarified.

That got a slash of a smile out of Lula. She relaxed. Not completely, but enough.

"You may not think killing Dominick is our goal," he said, "but it is very much my goal, Mother."

Cassia shook her head. "First, the child. First, the child comes home."

He didn't reply. Cassia pushed her chair back and stood. "Contact us. Before the full moon. If you want a room—"

"We don't," Lula said. "We'll let you know."

She didn't look at me, didn't have to. If Lula said we were done, we were done. I stood and snapped my fingers for Lorde. She chomped on the bone, pushed up, and walked over to us.

Lula and Lorde crossed the room and were out the door. I followed a little more slowly behind them, and was halfway to the door before I realized Abbi wasn't following us.

I turned. "Abbi?"

She was still sitting at the table. She waved at me. "Bye, Brogan. I'm staying with the witches."

"I don't think so," I said. "You're coming with us."

She gave me a frank look.

"No," she said. "I am staying here. I agreed to the terms already. I can help Rhianna. I'm going to do that no matter what anyone says. I'm powerful. With the full moon, I'm even more powerful. Bright like the sun."

I hesitated. Abbi was a deity. The witches loved her and practically fell over themselves to please her.

She had Hado to keep her safe or to come get us so we could keep her safe. But I still felt like I was leaving a child behind in a dangerous place.

Her eyes were moonlight silver and the power in

them was ancient. "*Go,*" I heard her say in my mind. "*Lula needs you.*"

I shook my head, but did as Abbi asked, following Lula into the night.

The air was heavy with stale heat that hadn't moved since June. I scanned the parking lot but didn't see Lu or Lorde. They might already be in the truck.

She could be gone, making deals with monsters, with hunters. Killing a vampire.

I strode past cars, trucks, and a trio of Vespas, the lights from the sodium lamps antiquing each vehicle with shades of sepia.

Lorde sat next to the truck, the blackness of her fur, eyes, nose making her almost invisible. The bone in her mouth caught the light. She wagged her tail as I came close enough to scratch behind her ears.

"Good girl. Where's Lula?"

Lorde whined, wanting in the truck so she could get back to chewing on her treat. She turned a dainty circle, inviting me to open the door for her.

We'd left the windows down, so I reached in and unlocked the door. "You seen Lula, girl?"

Lorde made a happy groaning sound and settled onto the seat. I gave her another ear scratch, then leaned back and patted the doorframe.

Options: Sit in the passenger's seat and hope Lula showed up, or get in the driver's seat and go look for her?

I didn't like driving, liked it even less at night. The broken wrist wasn't going to make it any more pleasant. But sitting in the shadows twiddling my thumbs wouldn't solve anything either.

So, driving it was.

I walked around the truck, checking the bed—no Lula—then opened the driver's door, feeling that uncanny tingle of someone watching me.

Light from the cab's overhead splashed a cleaner yellow into the night. If I hadn't been an obvious target before, I certainly was one now.

I hauled up into the driver's seat.

We kept a spare key on a magnet under the console, so I dug that out and put it in the ignition.

"Where are you, love?" I didn't expect her to hear me. With her speed, she could be a mile away by now.

I flicked on the headlights, and thought I heard a stirring in the branches of the tree, like a large bird or animal moving swiftly.

The passenger door flew open. I twisted, fist cocked.

"Hey, Brogan," said Raven from the open door.

"No."

"Yes. You and I need to talk." He swung into the cab, shut the door, then cooed at Lorde. "Who's this pretty girl? Aren't you a beautiful fuzzy wuzz? Yes, you are."

"What the hell are you doing here, in the witch's territory?"

"Right now? Petting your dog."

"Out."

Raven dug around between him and Lorde,

freeing the bone stuck there. "Lorde doesn't want me to leave, do you, girl?"

Lorde tapped her tail and nosed at his shoulder. He gave her the bone and scrubbed her head, strong fingers tracking furrows through her thick fur.

"Raven," I said, "out."

"Or, you could start driving," he said. "I know where Lula is."

Trickster. He'd say anything to get what he wanted.

"I don't believe you."

"Where's the trust?" He managed to sound offended. "I thought we were friends. Lorde and I are friends. Look, Lorde loves me."

"She loves anyone who feeds her treats."

"She doesn't love everyone," he said to Lorde. "Not even everyone who gives her treats." He threw me a look. "If she thought I was a danger or a threat, you'd know it."

"Says the trickster god. Out."

"But I haven't showed you where Lula is yet."

"Too late."

"Look, she's right there." He pointed past me. I couldn't help it. I glanced out the side window.

Lula was striding our way from the edge of the parking lot, her gaze locked on me. From the set of her shoulders, she was aware the god was in the truck too.

She paused on the other side of my door. "Brogan. Raven."

"I didn't invite him," I said.

"Perfect timing," Raven said. "I need to show both of you something."

"How about we say no? Again," I said.

"Then you won't have the information you need for making decisions about the witches, and the vampire, and the man who has the book."

I closed my eyes and sighed. "This better not be bullshit, Raven."

"Hurtful," Raven said. "I'll drive."

"No!" Lu and I said simultaneously.

"I'll drive," Lu said.

She was a better driver than me. Plus, if she drove, I'd have a hand free to throttle the god if the chance arose.

I got out and traded places with Lu, trying to catch her hand as I stepped past her. But she was just out of my reach, already swinging up into the truck.

Raven had scooted over so he was in the center of the bench seat, and Lorde hopped down and curled into her familiar place in the footwell.

I got in.

It was a tight fit.

"Cozy," Raven said.

"You could leave," I said, yet again.

"Abbi's fine, by the way," he said. "The coven think she's the best thing since the invention of the crock pot. She'll be safe while we're gone."

"I didn't ask about her," I said.

He tipped his head. "Still. I'm watching her. She has my feather."

I didn't want that to make me feel better, but it

did. "So, what's so damn important we have to see it now?"

"Up the road," he pointed in a generally north-west direction.

Lula shifted the truck into reverse. "How far?"

"A few miles. You'll know when we get there."

I hated the sound of that. But Lula didn't even glance my way. She just put the truck in drive and followed the road.

CHAPTER THIRTEEN

I had lost count of how many times Lula and I had driven Route 66. We'd been down this section of the road hundreds, if not thousands of times.

Still, the Route always looked different in the dark.

Felt different too.

Out here in the nothing lands between McLean and Amarillo, there were no lights to interrupt the night, nothing but a faded moon to pencil-sketch the plains rolling by on either side.

Raven was silent, watching the land slide past like he'd forgotten what the earth looked like at eye level.

I'd tried to get words out of him, but he'd only smiled, shook his head, and said, "Wait."

Twenty minutes in, we'd passed Allenreed and two rest areas.

Finally, Raven spoke. "Up there," he gestured north, "is where the coven's land ends. McClellan National Grasslands, or there about. And this…" he waited until we'd gone a bit farther, another five minutes or so, "...this is where the vampire territory begins."

Lula caught her breath, and I grunted like someone had just popped me in the sternum.

Like I said, we'd been down the Route hundreds of times. I'd been in spirit form for most of it, but that didn't mean I couldn't feel the living world.

Lula had been in flesh driving the Route. Being *thrawan* meant she was hyper-sensitive to vamps.

But this stretch of the Route had never felt so thick with the presence of vampires.

It was as if an invisible barrier had been pulled back and a hook had caught in my chest, dragging me backward, urging me to leave before the sharpened fangs got too close to my heart.

At the same time, all I wanted to do was go forward, lean into it, lean into that pain until I bled dry.

"What is that?" I asked.

"That," Raven said, "is a problem."

Lula slowed the truck, had been slowing it for some time. She pulled onto the shoulder, dust and gravel crunching under the wheels.

Her hands were locked on the wheel, knuckles bone white. She bit at her bottom lip, and the smallest drop of blood formed there.

"I can block it." Raven snapped his fingers, and I heaved a huge breath as if I'd just come up from the bottom of the ocean too quickly.

"Damnit," I coughed, "warn a man."

Lula swallowed, and swallowed, then wiped at her mouth with the back of her trembling hand.

I was shaking too.

"Sorry for the drama," Raven said, "but I needed you both to experience it so you would believe what I'm going to say next. You felt that, didn't you? You felt the beacon?"

"The hell kind of beacon is that?" I asked.

The hook in my chest, the call, the desire had been almost physical. Even though I hated the minutes I'd been in contact with it, it left an ache behind. An ache that made me want it again.

Fucking vampires.

"It's a…I suppose *geis* would be a good term," Raven said. "Compulsion works too."

"A compulsion from whom? To do what?" Even as I said it, I knew the answer.

It wasn't Raven who answered, though. It was Lula. "To fight Dominick for territory and power," she said. "Or die trying."

"That's correct," the god said. "Only other supernaturals can sense it. But really, it's a call to one person."

"Variance," Lula said.

Raven nodded. "Variance."

"Why is Dominick trying to lure him into a fight?"

"Variance was turned by Dominick," Raven said, "but Variance refuses to fall under his heel. Vampires —most—become less reasonable as time passes. Dominick is very old and has been ruling over the vampires in his territory for a very long time. With

Variance on his side, Dominick would move into the witches' territory, turning them and creating a powerful, new supernatural."

Vampire witches. The thought of magic-wielding vampires made chills run down my back.

"Does Dominick know that Variance is coming for his head?" I asked.

Raven nodded. "He's counting on it. He wants to break him, destroy the man who won't worship at his throne."

"Why wait for Variance to come to him?" I asked.

"He needs the power of his own territory," Lu said.

Again, Raven nodded.

"Does Dominick know we're here? That I'm here?" Lula asked.

"I don't think so," Raven said. "Not yet."

She shivered, her entire body shaking with it, but her gaze when she turned to look at Raven was steady. "Why is Dominick's call so familiar to me?"

Raven scrubbed a hand over his short hair and muttered under his breath.

His eyes seemed to dance with fire, with stars, with deadly, bright sparks of power. "Because he was turned by the monsters who attacked you nearly a hundred years ago."

For such a bombshell revelation, it was very quiet in the car.

Lula's only reaction was to lick the blood off her bottom lip.

I couldn't process the information, my brain too

scrambled with noise. So, I closed it off, pushed it away. Ignored it.

"Will Dominick's blood heal Rhianna?" I asked, needing something concrete on which to focus.

"It *might*," he admitted reluctantly. "I don't have a say over that outcome—by which I mean it is not strictly within my power to affect that outcome." He tapped his thumb on his knee.

"The witches are a wild card," he said. "They have very powerful magic on their hands in Bun Bun. She's good at this kind of thing, elixirs of life and whatnot."

"Then they don't need us." My voice was too loud in my ears. I wanted out of here. Wanted Lula out of here before she confronted Dominick—

—without me—

—before she fought him alone.

"You're a god," I went on. "Why don't you fly in there and steal back Rhianna? Why don't you take the vampire's blood?"

"Brogan," Raven said gently, as if he were trying to set me down carefully, trying to keep me from breaking along shattered lines where the glue wouldn't hold. "I am doing more than I should. I am meddling in something that Fate has set into motion. I am using my powers in a way...in a way that will almost certainly cost me."

Lorde got to her feet and put her head on my knees, looking up at me and whining softly.

"It's not the first time I've put a stone on the scales to make it tip the way I want," Raven said, "but this involves the spellbook. Anything—*everything*—to do with that book comes with consequences. To humans, supernaturals, gods, the universe."

"So, you won't get involved?" I said, "What good are you?"

"I never said I was good," Raven said. "But you're right. Someone needs to save the child. Variance can't. He'll be chewed up and spat out into little gobbets of flesh if he fights Dominick. He shouldn't leave the protection of the coven.

"But the book has resurfaced. Gods are battling on this earth. All wheels spin, and the beginning will always become the end. Dominick might have lost all sanity, but he has not lost his will to survive.

"It was always going to come to this," he said. "You've spent years searching for the monster who destroyed your lives. This is the beginning of that hunt's end. Through Dominick, his blood, his death, you will find the bindings that tie him to the monsters who nearly killed you both."

Lula closed her eyes and swallowed. "You're a trickster god," she said. "We can't take you at your word."

"No, you cannot. Whose word would you take?"

She shook her head.

"We need some time to think," I said. "Away from vampire territory."

Raven grinned. It was boyish and wicked. I had a moment to be glad he was on our side, or might be on our side, or at least wasn't currently against us.

"I know a place. Hang on." He snapped his fingers.

Nothing happened. It was still dark out. We were still in the truck.

But the air had changed. It smelled sweeter, for one thing, and more humid. Also, the wrong bugs were singing.

Lorde got up so she could look out the window, and *woof*ed.

"I would have done this earlier," Raven said, "but Bathin is a real pain in the ass, and wanted to meet you in Texas."

"What's the demon have to do with this?" I asked.

"Nothing if I have any say over it. But he has more contacts in Texas and likes doing business there."

"Brogan." Lula pointed.

A figure strode our way. She was at least six feet tall, wore overalls and a tank top. Her bare bronze skin absolutely glowed with tattoos.

Magic tattoos, because she was a Crossroads.

"Lula, Brogan," Ricky called out from a distance. "Would you like me to forcefully uninvite that god off my property?"

She rested the sledgehammer she carried on her shoulder. It glowed too.

"Ricky," Raven shouted. "Is that any way to say hello to an old friend?"

"Nope," she said. "Offer stands."

"It's fine," Lula said.

"We're in Missouri?" My brain hadn't caught up with reality. "Why are we in Missouri?"

"Are you hurt, Lula?" Ricky asked.

"She's fine," I yelled, "and so am I, thank you so much for asking." Yes, I was annoyed.

Lula pressed her palm over her mouth, and I thought she might be smiling. I wanted to keep that smile there.

"Did you just snap us across an entire state?" I demanded.

Raven wiggled his fingers. "Little bit of a rule breaker. You should see my dating profile. "Open the door, Brogan, the dog wants out."

"Lula?" Ricky said again.

Lu dropped her hand. Yeah, she'd been smiling.

Good. If we could laugh about this, we could maybe get back to calm heads and making solid plans.

"I'm fine, Ricky," Lu's voice was tinged with laughter. "Please tell me you have tea on."

Ricky hesitated, but only for a second. She was used to supernaturals showing up at her property at all hours asking for refuge.

She was one of the few supernatural neutral zones on Route 66. Being a Crossroads meant her home was a place where monsters and gods and mortals all played by the same rules.

Her rules.

She had a massive supply of magic and magical items stuffed into her near-sentient house, and usually spent her time negotiating peace between creatures that desperately needed it.

She was also Lu's best friend and someone I had been working hard not to think of as a rival for her affection.

While I sat there scowling, Lula opened her door.

Lorde took that as an invitation to jump up on my lap, then walk across a chuckling Raven and bolt out of the truck. She ran around Ricky's yard, dodging between Lula and Ricky, and getting pats as she zoomed by.

"All right then," Raven said. "This is our stop." He scooted across the seat to the driver's door.

"Why?" I asked. "Why here?"

"You trust her. Well, Lula trusts her. They're friends." He tapped the steering wheel, looking out into the darkness as if he could see universes. "I think she needs a friend right now. Especially if you two are going to do what has to be done."

I opened my mouth, but he nodded.

"Fight Dominick," he said, "save Rhianna. If we have any luck at all, we keep Variance alive and find that damn book so we can lock it away before it blows holes through everything we know about reality." He patted the steering wheel one last time and glanced at me. "Good talk."

With that, he slipped out of the truck and walked around it with his hands up and to his sides, as if showing the law he wasn't carrying any weapons.

"Ricky," he called out, "did you get taller? You're looking tall, my friend."

"You stole my hat, Raven. Don't think I forgot."

"Hat? What hat? Can you describe it?"

"Sure. It's felt, red, and has a brim you adjust with this finger." Ricky produced her middle finger, which made Raven hoot.

"I've missed you, Ricks. But I didn't take your hat."

He'd reached them, and they started across the yard to the house, which was now—magically—in view, every window glowing with light.

Lula had her arm across Ricky's back, leaning into her as they walked. Ricky's arm was around her shoulders.

Maybe Raven was right. Maybe Lula needed a friend now more than I knew.

"You comin' Brogan?" Ricky asked, as they reached the porch. "I've got pie."

I got a move on and strolled across the yard.

"I like pie," Raven said.

"Pie's only for nice people," Ricky said.

"Hey, I'm people."

"Oh, you very much are not." She stepped up to the porch and the whole house lit up with neon whorls and glyphs, the fire rippling down her arms. She held the door open, and Lula walked into the house past her.

Lorde zoomed by me, a wooly black shadow in the night. I reached down, only brushing the end of her tail before she rocketed away.

Ricky turned to Raven who had stopped at the foot of the stairs. "You know my rules," she said, "or do I need to remind you, god, of who and what I am?"

"I know your rules. No rocking the boat—any boat. All peace, love, and compromise. I know who you are, Crossroads."

"Neutral ground," she said. "No matter who shows up, no matter what shows up, this remains neutral ground. If you break that, the house will conjure up a cliff and I'll toss you out the window."

The house seemed to glow a little brighter. Lorde made another pass by me, this time slowing so I could run my fingers down her back.

"You should meet the Reed sisters," Raven mused. "I think you'd all get along great."

"That's not an agreement." She put her hands on her hips. "You will follow my rules, Raven."

"Yes. Agreed. Fine." Raven waved her words away. "I will follow your rules. While I'm in your house or on your property."

Ricky's tattoos flared soft pastel, and the house went back to a gentler glow. "All right." She gestured at the door. "Welcome to the Crossroads, Raven."

He grinned and mounted the stairs. "It's been a minute, hasn't it?"

"Since you've been hiding out? Yes. Why are you out in the world again?"

He pointed vaguely ahead and behind him. "This Route 66 thing needed attention."

Her gaze ticked up to me, because, apparently, I was this Route 66 thing.

"Something new I need to know?" she asked.

Raven paused before entering the house. "Old

things. Very old things. But we need new solutions now."

Ricky made a sound that might have been agreement. She knew about the book, and knew we were looking for it. Raven slipped past her into the place.

Lorde had finally run herself out and stopped next to me, panting happily.

"Go on in, girl," I said.

Lorde stopped for a quick head scratch from Ricky, then entered the house.

"Why are you here?" she asked me.

"That was Raven's idea."

"Oh?"

"He showed up at a diner with a demon. They were all about promises of a place where we can hide the spellbook. He said it would be safe. Out of the reach of gods and other supernaturals. Some library in Ordinary."

The house shivered, and I swore I heard a sweet little cooing sound.

Ricky smiled. "We like that library."

The cooing got louder and the scent of tea leaves, vanilla, and something that somehow smelled like lace doilies, wafted through the night.

"Is your house in love with a library?" I asked.

Ricky chuckled, almost too quietly to hear. "A little. It's okay. It's more of a long-distance relationship. They make it work."

And there was a new thing I'd just learned about the world.

"You okay, Brogan?" she asked, pointing at my braced arm, and then searching my face.

I pressed my good hand against the back of my sweaty neck. "We need to talk about Lula. I think I'm...I think something's wrong. Something I don't know how to fix."

"Are you coming in?" Raven asked from somewhere inside the house. "Or are you two going to spend all night gossiping and exchanging recipes?"

I heard something slide, like a book or a pot pushed off a shelf, then Raven yelped, and the item clattered to the floor.

"It wasn't an insult!" he yelled to the house. Something else skittered and slid. "All right, settle your shelves. I'm not touching anything. Ricky, talk to your house."

"Is she hurt?" Ricky asked me, ignoring the god.

I huffed out a breath, but I didn't know what to tell her. Yes? No? I met her understanding gaze and told her the truth. "I don't know."

She nodded once. "Come in, Brogan. Get something to eat and drink. Take your rest here. I can look at your arm if you want. We'll figure this out."

And with that welcome shepherding me, I walked past her into the quirky old building, and hoped she was right.

CHAPTER FOURTEEN

R icky's kitchen was homey and filled with fresh morning sunlight.

"Honky tonk witches?" she said over the sizzle of bacon. "Texas, right? Around McLean? I've heard of them. Is Cassia still the head of the coven?"

I grunted in affirmation and forked down the thick, fluffy biscuit covered in rich gravy. I chased it with hot black coffee and went for another bite. I was feeling a hell of a lot better today.

Sleep had dragged me down into dreamless darkness, the comfortable bed with a floral quilt Lula had admired, and the soothing quiet of the house keeping me there. My wrist was sore, but only when I tried to move it. I'd woken this morning with a much clearer head.

"Haven't met her son," she said. "Variance? Or the granddaughter." She placed three strips of bacon on a small plate with bite-size fruit and a muffin-sized quiche. "I haven't even heard of Dominick,

which is odd. I eventually hear about all the supernaturals."

Raven was out in the yard throwing bread at the
birds that sat in the old fruit tree. They were
squawking down at him like he was a predator in their
territory. He was trying to convince them to eat the
bread and laughing at their noise like he was in on the
jokes. Lorde was out there with him, lying in the sun.

"I'm not saying you should know," I said, pushing
my empty plate away. "I didn't come here to blame
you. But I think…hate to admit this…I think the god
had a good idea in bringing us here. Lula needed the
rest."

I nodded toward the upstairs where Lu was still
sleeping. She'd gone straight to the room, taken a
shower, then crawled into bed before I'd even made it
up the stairs.

"And you needed some food." She eyed my plate.
"Because you haven't eaten in a…month?"

I shrugged. "You're a good cook."

"That sounded like a compliment, Gauge."

"Take it as you want," I said, full and feeling
magnanimous.

"I will. But I don't think a sleepover is the only
reason you're here."

"No. We need information. About the witches, the
vampires, the book."

"Lucky for you information is another thing I'm
good at." She picked up the plate and gave me a
smile, like we were friends. Which, really, I thought we
might be.

Lula loved her. I was grateful she'd given Lula a place to come over all the years I'd been nothing but a spirit. I was grateful she was someone Lu could talk to, laugh with, cry with.

"But first," Ricky said, "I'm taking her breakfast. Unless you want to?"

"She'd love to see you."

"Brogan, I…" She stopped then shook her head. "We'll figure this out."

"I know." I cleared my throat and changed subjects. "You wouldn't happen to know Lula's favorite dessert?"

"Of course I do. It's…wait. Do you? You don't? Why don't you know your wife's favorite dessert?"

"I have reasons."

"All those years watching her, and you never paid attention to what she ate?"

"Hey, I thought we were friends."

"Doesn't mean I can't find you absolutely hilarious. A hundred years. You had nearly a hundred years to notice."

I scowled, and she laughed her way out of the kitchen.

I didn't have anything to do, and was feeling restless, so I took my dishes to the sink and ran the hot water. I got enough soap going the bubbles reached up to my elbow.

The very ordinary monotony of scrubbing, washing, rinsing, stacking was a lot more complicated with only one working hand. But I got the hang of it and soon, the repetition calmed me.

The scent of artificial lemon mixed with the aroma of the breakfast Ricky had cooked up: eggs, bacon, gravy, salt, grease, and sweet buttered dough. I took a deep breath and felt my shoulders drop.

We were safe here. Could stay here if we wanted. I knew Ricky would let us. The house had power. Ricky had power. Enough we could withstand anything the vampires threw at us. Probably anything the witches threw at us.

But gods knew about this place. Atë could know about it, or that we were here. I didn't want to bring a war to Ricky's home, to her place of safety.

It might be a Crossroads, a magical point along Route 66 that contained and could access many powerful things, but it was not a fortress.

Even Crossroads could be destroyed.

No, if we were going to finish this, if we were going to get the book and help save Rhianna, if we were going to kill Dominick and bring the witches his blood, we couldn't stay here.

This was a place of rest, not battle.

"We won't bring the fight here," I told the house. "We don't want Ricky or you to be involved. I don't know what Raven wants out of this. Not really. But I'm sorry he involved you."

The house seemed to be listening, seemed to be waiting. I wasn't connected to it the way Ricky was, but it could make itself known when it wanted. Talking to it was a little like knowing a very large creature was watching you from just beyond the tree line.

I could hear Ricky's and Lula's voices upstairs, a

buzzy, happy murmur. The room was far enough away from the kitchen, I shouldn't be able to hear them.

That would be the house's doing, then, letting me know they were okay.

"Ricky's a good friend." I placed a plate on the towel I'd spread on the countertop and used another towel to finish drying it. "Thank you for being here for her."

The house went silent, the voices no longer in range. The birds had stopped giving Raven hell, and I could hear his slow sweet whistle as he called back to them in their own song.

The cupboard to my left flew open.

"Holy mother—"

A cookbook slammed down onto the counter, and a puff of wind blew into the room—even though the doors and windows were shut. The book flipped open to a page near the back.

"This better be good," I muttered to the house. "About gave me a heart attack."

The page had one recipe: STRAWBERRY ANGEL FOOD CAKE. The recipe was smudged with oil and stained red at the corner. Someone had dropped a strawberry on it, but the text was still legible.

Recipes that showed wear and tear were almost always the best ones. Still, it took me a minute to understand what I was looking at.

"This is her dessert, isn't it? Lula's favorite." I placed my palm in the middle of the page, holding the book down, not wanting it to go anywhere.

Memories of when we'd first begun our journey on the Route popped like camera flashes behind my eyes. Those were dark, uncertain days. But every summer she'd make strawberry angel food cake.

She didn't always eat it, especially not at first when she had been grappling with how to survive as half-vampire. But she would mix it up and bake it, just that small moment of normality giving her peace.

I couldn't remember when she'd stopped making it, or why. But yes, the house was right. It had been her favorite dessert when we were alive, and for years afterward.

"Hang on. Let me find paper and pencil so I can copy this down."

There was the feeling of a massive eye roll, which wasn't something a house should be able to convey.

Then a drawer that had held silverware a minute ago, when Ricky had been in the kitchen, slid open. No silverware. Nothing in the drawer but a single index card.

I picked it up.

It was the strawberry angel food cake recipe hand-written in a tight, legible print.

I grinned and tucked the note card into my pocket. "Thank you."

"You're welcome," Raven said, coming through the door. "What are you thanking me for?"

"I'm not."

"Huh. Feels like you should. Is Ricky up with Lula?"

"Not sure that's your business."

The house gave me another eye roll.

Yeah, I knew Raven had agreed to play by the rules, but that didn't change my opinion on trickster gods.

Raven strolled over to the table and rested a hand on the back of a chair. "Don't worry," he said. "The house has its thumb pressed down so hard on me, I can't exhale without its permission. I feel like a game of darts. Want to play?"

"No."

But the house shifted. Instead of the wall with a door that opened on the back yard, there was a wall with a dart board.

Two sets of darts waited on the table.

Crow picked the set with black feathers, leaving the white-feathered darts behind. He took his place several paces away from the target.

"You know how to play, don't you?" he asked.

"I've played darts, Raven."

"Want to make a friendly wager?"

"No. I want the truth." I picked up the darts with my good hand and stood next to him.

He nodded toward the target. "All right." A flick of the wrist and the dart landed just below the bulls-eye. "Ask."

"Can you lie to us while you're here?" I lined up, threw the dart. Bullseye.

He made a small, impressed sound. "Sure. Lying doesn't break any of Ricky's rules."

"Are you lying to us now?"

The corner of his mouth hooked upward.

"Probably? But not about everything." He threw the next dart. Close, but no cigar. "Be more specific," he said.

"Is Dominick the vampire who attacked us? Who made us…what we are now?"

"Brogan, I wasn't there when it happened. I didn't see it happen."

I threw the next dart. Bullseye.

Raven whistled. "I'm glad I didn't set a wager on this game."

"The witches told us Dominick was the one who turned us, then said they were lying. You told us he was turned by the monster who attacked us. Which is the truth, Raven?"

He took extra time lining up his shot. Then, finally, quietly, "I don't think Dominick is the monster who attacked you, no."

He threw the dart. Bullseye.

"Why?" I still held my dart, waiting.

"Because the monster who attacked you and Lula was turned into a monster by Atë." He raised an eyebrow at my expression. "Oh, you didn't know that, did you? She made it into what it is—vampire, mostly —but twisted it into her image, all humanity and soul stripped. That kind of…influence from a god is difficult to survive. And yet."

"It's still out there," I breathed.

It was cool in the house, even with the morning heat setting in. Still, sweat trickled down my spine. All these years Lula had been looking for it, I'd thought it was still out there. But there was a part of me that had begun to wonder if it had died, been killed. Not even monsters live forever.

"I think so, yes. Dominick is a vile, cruel, power-hungry creature. But he is not the vile, cruel, power-hungry creature that attacked you."

"Fuck." I threw the dart—bullseye—and turned to him. "Do you know where it is?"

Crow bit his bottom lip, and I could see the power in him banked and burning like black-feathered flame.

"I think you will know, Lula will know, if you kill Dominick. I think that connection between them will show you where the monster is hiding. But my guess? Atë is protecting it, keeping it away, maybe even away from this earthly realm."

I filed that particular horror away for another time. "Is it true Atë can't use the book without Lula and me?"

"Atë has never understood mercy. She had never seen the benefit in sharing the universes with some-thing other than herself. She was rejected by the gods, her power refused a place in the spellbook. She wanted to be the only god who could touch it, who could use it. We wouldn't let that happen."

"I've seen her touch it," I said. "She had it in her hands."

"Did she? Or was that an illusion?"

I replayed that time in the farmhouse. When Lula had been trapped beneath the floor, when I had just come back from the dead and was trying to save her. I wasn't sure, couldn't be sure if Atë had actually held the book in her hands.

"Gods are very good at illusions," Raven said. "Even gods who aren't tricksters. So, yes. I am very certain she can't use the book without Lula's hands and your voice.""That has to be bullshit."

"It's not. You know what's bullshit? You throwing three bullseyes without even trying. You are a hustler, Brogan Gauge. If you ever get tired of the Route, you could make good money. Hell, you could make good money on the Route."

"I don't care about darts. Tell me everything. Any information you have on the monster that turned us."

He stared at the ceiling a moment and nodded, as if dragging up old memories. "Lula's not a full vampire, is she?"

"It's called a *thrawan*," Lu said, walking into the kitchen. Her hair was braided back, but still damp from a shower. She'd changed into jeans, a tank top and boots—her standard traveling clothes.

She didn't expect us to be staying here long.

The wall changed back into a wall with a door to the outside, the dartboard and darts disappearing in a flash.

"We know I'm not a full vampire," she added.

Raven meandered over to the table and dropped down into a chair.

"Yes. *Thrawan*. But the monster that turned you *thrawan* isn't fully vampire either. It's god-turned, chaos-blooded, mutated. It was Atë's way of creating a tool she needed: hands that can touch the book and a voice that can cast its spells."

Ricky wandered into the kitchen and put dishes in the sudsy water. She made a small, interested noise.

I didn't want to believe Raven, but this wasn't something we could change. We were a hundred years too late to change any of this.

"I'm the hands," Lula breathed out, and the world was loud again, real again. "I can touch it. I *have* touched it. It knocked Brogan out when he tried. It repels everyone out who tries to touch it."

Raven tapped his nose in agreement. "It chooses who can touch it. That was the protection woven into it. But there are ways around its protections, because there are always ways around things like that. Ghouls, for instance, can slip through certain god-placed loopholes. Ask me how I know, and I'll tell you a funny story about a car falling out of the sky."

"I don't…" I cleared my throat. "There must be others who can handle the book. More than just Lula."

Lula was looking at me oddly.

Raven was looking at me oddly too. But he shrugged. "Well, like I told you at the diner, there is one more. You," he said simply. "You're the voice."

CHAPTER FIFTEEN

There was a cool breeze blowing through the kitchen, just a soft breath of a thing whisking over my forehead and face.

"I was dead—that monster killed me, turned me into nothing but a ghost," I said. "How could I be the voice?"

Raven picked up a cup of coffee and drank, refusing to answer me.

"You weren't a ghost," Ricky said. "And no, you weren't barely a ghost, either. When you were angry, really angry, you moved the world, Brogan. We could hear you. Even through the veil between the living and dead."

"It makes sense," Lula said.

"It doesn't make sense," I said. "No damn god is going to halfway kill me and you just so she can make us into puppets she can control."

Raven *tsk*ed, the softest of sounds. "Gods always get what they want. You know that. Gods will go to any extreme it takes to get something they really want. Something like revenge, and Atë wants revenge on all the gods who wouldn't let her play with their spellbook."

I was pacing, couldn't hold still. "This can't... Why?" I heard the volume of my words but couldn't find the dial to turn it down. "Why us? There are millions of people, *billions*. Why us?"

Silence ticked between the songs of birds warbling outside. A flock had found Crow's offering and were making their way through the field.

Lorde walked through the door, warm from the sun, wagging her tail. She leaned against my leg, a fuzzy, stalwart presence. I stopped pacing and dropped my hand into her soft fur.

Lu stared out the kitchen window, her eyes the palest color of honey. I couldn't read her expression.

Ricky frowned, her palms braced on the edge of the countertop, arms locked straight behind her. "It's a good question, Raven. Why them?"

He put his cup down. "You have very strong souls," he said kindly, the voice of a father, an uncle, a brother who was trying to catch your shoulder and guide you through the darkness of a frightening place. "Strong enough that a piece of your soul was torn from you and fused to Lula's. Strong enough a piece of her soul was torn from her and fused to you. Yin. Yang. She lived, mostly. You died, mostly. Not many can survive that. It's probable not many did."

Ricky swore softly at that revelation.

"You and Lula survived. Because you refused to

stop," Raven went on. "You refused to stop loving, to stop hoping. Even when it seemed there was no tomorrow left for you."

"The watch." Lu turned. Her amber eyes were clear. "It helped," she said. "To touch you. To see you."

I moved to her, unable to deal with the distance between us. I put my arm around her, and she leaned into me.

"I don't think Atë expected you would have the watch," Ricky said.

Raven's smile was wide. "No, she did not. That was a nice bit of luck, a very special bit of magic."

"Did you send it to them, Raven?" Ricky asked.

"Wish I had. Wish I'd done more. But I wrote off Atë years ago and forgot that damn spellbook even existed."

"Forgot?" Ricky said. "How do you forget a spellbook full of god power?"

"It was a lark, Ricky, a romp. And not the first or last I've been a part of."

"A romp?" She scoffed. "It can destroy worlds. Destroy lives. Gods! I don't think there's a single creature more short-sighted or self-absorbed."

"There isn't," Raven agreed. "I've been around for a long time. How could I *not* have forgotten powerful things? And, unfortunately," he nodded toward us, "how could I not have overlooked important things?"

"Maybe because you care about them?" Ricky said. "And now that the book matters to you, now that you want it, you're sticking your beak into other people's business."

"I stick my beak into people's business because I like my beak there. This—this is definitely personal."

"Because someone touched your precious spell in the book and dropped a car out of the sky?" she asked.

"Because someone used a single spell—*mine*—out of that damned book to threaten the people I love. To threaten my home."

The god grew darker, shadows a feathered blackness around him.

"*That* is why I am breaking a few minor, very small, rules about what I can and cannot do inside or outside Ordinary, with or without Fate, and shutting this problem down permanently."

Ricky blew a raspberry. "Get in line. Cupid's got dibs on the book."

"Cupid doesn't know how to keep it safe."

"I'd like to be there when you tell him that," she said.

"I can arrange it, but I *don't* think you would like it."

She pushed away from the counter. "So, if we believe you're telling the truth…"

"I am. Because it benefits me to do so."

"…then Atë created the vampire-monster who turned Lula and half-killed Brogan."

"Yes."

"Then is Dominick that creature?" Ricky asked.

Lula inhaled and held that breath. I tightened my

arm around her. I knew the answer. I knew it wasn't what she wanted to hear.

"No. I don't think so, no."

The tension in Lula changed, and she released the breath.

"That isn't why we're going to help the witches," I said. "If we do it—fight Dominick, kill Dominick—it's because there's a child's life on the line. A child in danger isn't something we walk away from."

Raven spread his fingers. "I know. But I brought you here for Ricky to corroborate my information. She and the house are free to check if what I say is correct."

"We will," Ricky promised.

"What about the hunter, Hatcher?" I said.

Lula didn't lean away from me, but I could tell she didn't like this change of subject.

"He touched the book," I said.

Silence.

"He held the book, Raven," I insisted, "back in Illinois. He took it from us and shot Lorde."

The house darkened, and I heard a distant growl.

"Calm down," Ricky said. "Lorde's fine. She's right over there."

The growling stopped, but the house lights were still darkened. Then a pile of toys and chew bones popped into existence next to Lorde.

Lorde yipped happily and sniffed her way through the offerings. She chose a squeaky ear of corn the size of a small country.

"Your point?" Raven asked.

Lorde chewed hard, and the corn squealed. She dropped it and yipped, batting it with her feet.

"That means Lula isn't the only one who can touch it," I said.

Raven shrugged. "The book chooses who can touch it. But what you're trying to point out? That Atë can just use someone like Hatcher to access the power in that book? No. The hunter would not work for her."

"Why?"

"He'd probably explode."

I gave him a look.

"I am capable of telling the truth, Brogan. Hatcher, if he's human, or most other creatures, has only one soul. But you two have two souls, and each is welded to the other." He jammed his fingers together and made a fist with both hands. "It gives you endurance. Makes you stronger. Strong enough to be a tool for a god. Well, not for me," he unlocked his fingers. "I don't use tools. I'm more hands on. After all, the dirty work is half the fun."

"You asked us to bring the book to you," Lula said.

"Ordinary. I asked you to bring it to Ordinary."

"I don't see you out there tracking it down," I said.

"I think the witches have a line on it," he said. "Haven't I mentioned that yet?"

"Isn't that convenient," Ricky said. "The witches find the book while Lula and Brogan put their necks on the line saving a child from a vampire who is spoiling for a fight. Sounds like you're gilding a bear trap, Raven."

"Or I'm helping to get the book into the right hands, and that comes with risk. Sometimes you have to trust someone untrustable, Ricky."

"Like you."

"Life demands risk. You know that."

Ricky had found a glass of lemonade and took a drink. The ice in the glass clattered. "You're asking them to take a hell of a lot of a risk, Raven."

"We can save the girl," Lula said. "We will save her," she said to me, "that was never the question. If we get Dominick's blood, will the witches need more than their power to cure Rhianna? Will they need more to cure Variance?"

Raven looked at Ricky, and Ricky set down her lemonade. "Let me do some research." She walked out of the kitchen toward her study.

"Remember," Raven called after her. "He's a witch vampire, not vampire witch."

"How can I forget something I just learned ten minutes ago? And stop feeding the birds. You'll attract geese, and they'll crap all over my lawn."

"I know you were talking to Brogan," Lula said, "but I need to hear it from you. Do you think his blood will cure Rhianna?"

Raven rubbed at his jaw. I had a second to consider just how old of a creature he was, and just how many things he had experienced, known, and forgotten.

"If I had to guess," he began in that low, kindly

voice, "I'd put my money on the witches finding a way to bring her and her father back to his humanity."

She nodded and looked up at me. "I'll go ask Ricky for weapons."

"Good," I said, "good."

She drew away. Then it was just me and Lorde and Raven in the kitchen. A headache settled behind my eyes. I wanted a shower and to sleep for a month. No, I wanted a vacation. Somewhere away from the Route. Away from all of this.

"You'll want to get that," Raven said.

The phone rang. There was now an old-fashioned, yellow landline telephone attached to the wall.

"It's Ricky's phone," I said.

"Ricky's busy."

"Then you get it," I said.

"I'm busy too. *So* busy." He kicked his feet up into the empty chair and gulped down more coffee.

"For the love of—" I picked up the phone. "Hello."

"Hi, Brogan, hi!" Abbi was breathless, happy.

"Did Ricky make moon cookies? I love moon cookies. And is Valentine there? I bet Valentine's there. Oh, Cassia says hello. She wants to wave at you, no, she wants cookies too. No, oh…the phone?"

The sound of the phone being handled crackled through the line.

"We have information on Rhianna. A way to reach her," Cassia said.

The pounding in my head got worse. "How?"

"We are witches," she said. "We used magic, guided by the Moon Rabbit."

"I'm very powerful! Very bright!" Abbi shouted so close to the receiver, I winced. "Like the sun!"

"How can she be reached?" I clarified.

"I'd rather not say over the phone. But we need to act quickly. Tonight…"

"Because it's a full moon, and that's better than a full sun!" Abbi said.

"…tonight is our chance," Cassia agreed. "Can you be here?"

She didn't ask where we were. I assumed Abbi had told her the number to dial for Ricky, but she might not know we'd been god-snapped to Missouri.

I knew what Lula would say. We'd already decided to help save Rhianna, even if Dominick wasn't the monster we'd been hunting. "We'll be there."

"Yay!" Abbi cheered. "Can you bring moon cookies?"

"Abbi," I said.

"Thank you," Cassia said.

She ended the call. I hung the receiver on the hook, turned, and leaned against the wall, thumping my head against it once.

Lula strolled back into the room, took one look at me, glanced at the god, then back at me. "News?"

"The witches have new information. They need us there tonight," I said. "They said the clock's ticking."

She motioned at Raven. "We don't have time to drive. You'll need to snap us back to Texas."

"Do I?"

Ricky walked into the room and deposited various magical weapons onto the table. "This is important, god. Get a move on. Make with the snapping."

For the first time, I saw a glimmer of annoyance flash across his face, but he covered it with a droll smile.

"Oh, is *this* an important issue? Something we should pay attention to? Something a god would take time *out of his vacation*—a much deserved vacation by the way—to deal with? It's *that* kind of important? Do tell."

She just sorted weapons by size. "So much drama. Like you've done any serious work in decades."

"I've worked."

"Uh-huh."

"I'll have you know I run a very...well moderately...well not *un*successful shop in a quirky little tourist town."

"Wow," she said, the sarcasm just oozing. "Do you turn on the OPEN sign all by yourself every day?"

He waved his hand in the air. "I have people for that."

I joined Lula and Ricky at the table and considered the weapon options.

Ricky picked up a knife, a spool of thread, and a ring and handed them to me.

"Knife with origin soil from the original vampire, which isn't ideal—I'd prefer to have the soil of Dominick's homeland, but I don't have that. Still, this will give it more kick against any vamp you find.

Spool of thread so you don't get lost. Ring for speed. Best we can do on short notice."

I put the ring on my good hand, stuck the thread in my pocket, and held onto the sheathed knife, since it was going to take two good hands to attach it to my belt. "Thank you."

"Lu?" Ricky asked. "Choose your poison."

Lula already had knives, guns, and other weapons back in the truck. "Defensive, I think," she said.

Ricky pointed at a leather bracelet with dark stones. "Good for cloaking. How about a few explosives?"

And oh, how my wife smiled. "Lay it on me."

Ricky handed her a string of what looked like acorns, although they were bright blue and too large to actually be acorns. "These should do you."

Lula took them. "Thank you."

"I should come with you," Ricky said.

"No," Lu shook her head. "Your power is here. And what you've done," she lifted her hand to indicate the place of rest, the friendship, and then pointed at the table and the remaining magical deadly bits and bobs, "is more than enough. Is everything."

"Anytime. I am here. We are here for you. And if you need me, call. Oh, and the house says take this to the witches." Ricky handed Lu a flat box. "It's the diary of a very powerful witch. She did a lot of healing, including vampire bites."

Lu took it. "Thank you."

Ricky pulled her into a hug. When she released Lu, I was there, waiting for my turn.

"Well, well," she said, accepting a hug, and hugging me back. "Be careful," she whispered. "Don't die."

I gave her a small squeeze to indicate that was the plan.

CHAPTER SIXTEEN

"A hundred miles out," I said for the millionth time. "He's a god. He could have dropped us at the honky tonk's front door."

Lula was driving, Lorde with her new favorite corn toy, lying between us.

Raven was nowhere to be seen.

"One snap and he could have had us in the bar."

"Maybe he just wanted to give you a hundred miles to complain before we got there," she suggested.

I huffed and squinted out the window. The landscape was dried out, life and color sucked down by summer's fangs. I was tired, I was hot—had I ever not been hot?—the headache constant now.

Hollow. I felt as hollow as the landscape.

Strawberry angel food cake. How had I forgotten that? Ricky had remembered. Even the stinking magical house had remembered. But me? No.

On the heels of that thought, I knew I was kidding myself. Had been kidding myself for years.

There wasn't going to be a birthday party. Because she and I didn't get to live lives filled with normal joys. She and I didn't have a life with time for candles and cakes.

We weren't people anymore. Those kinds of happiness weren't ever coming our way.

Lu eased the truck into the honky tonk's parking lot where half a dozen people lingered beneath the shade of the tree on the corner.

A small figure burst out of the group and ran toward the truck, waving.

"Hi, oh, hi!" Abbi popped up next to my window before Lu had even put the vehicle in park. "We really do need help. Did you bring Valentine? I don't see Valentine. Is he hiding? Is Ricky here too?"

"No ghost, no Ricky," I said. "Just me and Lula."

Abbi stuck out her bottom lip, then brightened. "You came! That's good. Isn't that good?"

Her words hit like a small hammer on a steel pipe. Just a constant ringing rattle, echoed by pain. My headache was ramping up enough my stomach was about to get in on the act.

"It is," I said. I fumbled with the door and stepped out into the heat. My lungs were on fire, and the sunlight speared my eyes, blinding me.

I blinked hard and dark spots swarmed to block out the edges of my vision. Abbi had either stopped talking, or the whole world had gone quiet and buzzy.

"Inside." Lula cupped my shoulder and took my arm. She guided me toward the building.

I was going to argue, but if I opened my mouth I'd start heaving.

Then the light was gone, the heat was gone, all of it blacked out as we crossed into the Honky Tonk.

Cool, blessedly cool air enveloped me, and I shivered, not sweating, but suddenly too cold.

"Sit." Lu pushed me down into a chair. "Drink slowly." She placed a glass, wet, cold, in my hand.

I lifted it, drank. The water was sweet shade and soft rain. I wanted to gulp, but she squeezed my shoulder. "Slowly, Brogan. We have time."

So, I took small sips and closed my eyes. Just for a moment, just until the hammering faded.

Soon her hand was gone, and a cool cloth draped across the back of my neck, leeching away the heat there.

I must have made a sound, because the cloth lifted and came down again, the other side cooler.

She pressed on the cloth, then dragged it over my shoulder and down my arm. I would know that touch anywhere, had spent a hundred years craving it.

There wasn't a song playing, just the distant pleasant chatter of people caught in conversation. I couldn't say how many of the witches were here. At the moment, I didn't care.

The chair next to me pulled outward.

I opened my eyes and watched Lula sit, a glass of lemonade in her hand. She placed it on the table in front of me, the box with the witch's diary that Ricky had wanted us to give to Cassia in the center of the table. Lu opened her other hand and offered me two small pills.

"Aspirin. For your head."

"It's fine. I'm fine."

Her eyebrows rose, then the corner of her mouth lifted, bringing with it a full smile. "Ricky thinks we are the two most stubborn mules on the earth."

"Has she met every mule on earth?" I plucked the pills from her hand, popped them in my mouth, and washed them down with lemonade.

"She says she can prove it with statistics."

I grunted and set the glass back down.

She placed her hand over mine. I matched our palms, catching her fingers. "Lula…"

"No, me first," she said. "I'm sorry. I've been…" She pressed her lips into a thin line, then took a breath and met my gaze.

"I've been afraid," she said. "About a lot of things. How to keep you safe—us safe. I know, I know."

She shifted in the chair, and I distantly registered music was playing now. The smell of hops and an orange-scented cleaner filled the air.

But right now, always, the only person I could see, the only person in the world for me, was Lula.

"I've missed you," I said, squeezing her fingers gently. "I don't like arguing. Thank you for coming back to me. For being with me. All these years, my love."

She huffed and looked away. When she turned back, tears glittered in her eyes.

"I have been right next to you," she said. "I haven't left you. Haven't gone anywhere."

I just held her gaze. She glanced away again and dashed a hand across her eyes.

"I know," I said, finding the exit off this stage. "We've both done the best we could. We both worry about the other. But we trust each other to make good decisions. To be strong and safe." I waited a moment. "Right?"

"Of course we trust," she said. "But I worry. Your wrist…"

"What about my wrist?"

"It could have been so much worse."

"It could have. But it wasn't. We'll take that as a win and go forward. But," I said, "if going forward means we're alone or apart, then you and I will walk away from all of this—gods, witches, demons, and devils be damned."

She nodded again, then wiped her fingers on her pants. "We do this together. I won't lose you, Brogan Gauge."

I drew her in as I leaned toward her. "You have never, not for a moment, lost me. I'm not going to let that happen. And neither will you."

Then she was there, everywhere, and I was lost in her, in the scent of her perfume, in the softness of her lips.

The kiss began as a question and warmed into memories, promises. It ended slowly, gently, with *yes, forever, yes.*

"Yay," Abbi said, not loud, but right next to me.

"They're happy again. Good. Now we can go steal the little girl and poke the bad vampire."

I felt Lula's smile on my lips and opened my eyes. Her gaze was golden, sunlight and life, and I smiled as I fell again, always, helplessly in love with her.

"Wanna go poke a bad vampire?" I whispered.

She didn't draw away, so close she was all I could see, all I wanted to see. "I want to save a child," she said. She squeezed my fingers, and then gently unwove our hands. She moved her chair closer and sat back.

Her hand rested on my thigh, and I inhaled a full breath, finally feeling home again.

"You still like strawberries, right?" I asked her.

"I'll always love strawberries."

"Me too," Abbi said. "I love strawberries."

"Why?" Lula asked.

The door opened, exhaling a wash of heat and the scent of hot tar and dust. Cassia walked in, the heels of her boots matching the rhythm of the song playing in the background.

"Thank you for coming." She wore practical clothing—denim jeans, a light tank top under a light overshirt. Her sunglasses were propped on her head. She pulled out a chair and sat with us at the table.

Her gaze lingered on the box on the table, but she didn't ask.

"We plan to save Rhianna tonight." She pressed her hand on the table, fingers splayed. "Dominick knows we will use the full moon to increase our magic.

He knows we will come for Rhianna, so we don't have much in the way of surprise."

"You know where she is?" I asked.

"At his ranch, near Amarillo. It's huge, though, with enough land around it, anyone can disappear out there. Lots of people have."

The music rolled into a different song, something about rivers and lost loves.

Variance was suddenly next to our table. I flinched, then scowled, angry at my reaction to the vampire's speed.

"I can take you to him," he said.

"That sounds like a terrible plan," I said. "He wants you there. Wants you close enough that he can kill you."

"Neither of you know the layout of the ranch." His gaze ticked to me, and the fury there was palpable. "I was there for three months."

"Do you know where he's keeping her?" I asked.

"She is *my* daughter." He didn't raise his voice, but the words hit.

Vampire.

"Your daughter's going to need a father to come home to." I leaned forward. "If all you're doing is getting yourself killed, nobody wins."

Cassia cleared her throat. "We have an inside man. That is what we needed to tell you. He's agreed to guide you in tonight."

Variance's pupils were pinpoint, a killer's focus, and his face was stone. "Try and stop me from saving my child."

"How about I try to stop you from walking into a trap?" I said. "How about I try and stop you from committing suicide?"

"Variance and I will go," Lula said. "He knows the place. And Rhianna will know him and trust him."

"You mean he goes with us," I countered. "I'm not staying behind."

All eyes turned to me, and before I could say anything, Abbi spoke.

"You have a broken wrist, heat exhaustion, and you're slow. Like, I'm a rabbit and, you know, magic, so I'm fast. Vampires are fast, too, and so is Lula. None of us have broken anythings." She wrinkled her nose. "And you're slow."

"I'm not that slow. My wrist is fine. I'm going." I picked up the lemonade and drained the glass. There was not a single chance in hell I would let Lula walk into a nest of vampires without me at her side.

The silence in the room told me exactly what they all thought about that.

"We have weapons," Lula told Cassia in such a way that I knew she and I would be having words over my decision later. "We're ready when you are."

"Then that's it," Cassia said. She stood and touched Variance's arm, but he didn't respond. Probably because he was still wondering if killing me might be a good warmup for the night.

"The four of you will find Rhianna and bring her home. Once she is safely on her way here, get Dominick's blood. We will do all we can to help, but we will have to do it from our land. If we step into his territory, he will know."

"Wait." Lula lifted the box and offered it to Cassia. "A friend of our says this contains information that can help heal vampire bites."

Cassia's eyebrows lifted, but she accepted the box. "Thank you." For some reason she looked my way. "That is…thank you." Then she waved, and a few people standing by the bar started toward us.

"I don't like you, Brogan Gauge," Variance said, not done with the fight.

I shrugged. "I don't care."

His gaze slipped to Lula, and whatever he found there didn't make him any happier.

"Variance," Cassia warned. "This is done now."

He turned and strode to the bar.

"What kind of weapons do you have?" Abbi asked. "Are they Ricky's?"

"I'll show you," Lula said.

"Go ahead," Cassia said to Abbi and Lu, as a woman and man paused by our table. The woman handed Cassia her doctor's bag, and the man spread out a cloth filled with dried herbs. "We have a few loose ends to tie off."

"I'll get out of your way." I made to stand.

"No. Sit. You're part of our loose ends. Let's see if we can finish healing your wrist."

I was about to argue, but Lula threw me a look.

"All right," I said. "What do you need me to do?"

CHAPTER SEVENTEEN

It took fifteen minutes of spell writing, herb burning, and magic chanting for my wrist to feel almost as good as new. Then I was firmly encouraged (ordered) to get some sleep before the evening's work.

Cassia and her coven didn't give me another thought, completely ignoring me as they went about their preparations for the rise of the full moon.

I shuffled off to one of the small bedrooms attached to the back of the place, following my gut instinct for where Lula might be.

I knocked on the door once, then tried the handle. It was unlocked, so I opened it.

Lula lay on her side on the wooden-framed double bed. Lorde was curled up in a pile of pillows on the throw rug that covered most of the floor. A ceiling fan made lazy turns, stirring the cooler air the air conditioner pushed out with a soft hum.

"There you are," I said softly, even though it was only the three of us in the room.

"Here I am," she replied just as quietly.

She watched me walk into the room, her gaze ticking down to my unwrapped wrist, then back to my face.

"All better." I wiggled my fingers for proof. "Mind if I join?"

"Did they send you here for a nap?"

"They threatened to turn me into a frog if I didn't."

She smiled, then scooted back to the edge, making room for me. "Come on over, Kermit."

I opened my mouth and made a half-hearted wave of hands to mimic the Muppet.

That got a huff of a laugh out of her, and I felt some of the tension, the fear in me, ease.

I settled onto the bed, springs creaking and popping as I lay down to face her, my boots hanging off the end.

I hadn't expected a high-quality mattress, but it was surprisingly comfortable.

"This is nice," I said, the fatigue of the last few days, weeks, weighing heavily on me.

She hummed and adjusted her feet, resting the toes of her shoes against my shins.

"I don't want you to go tonight," she said. "To find Rhianna. I want you to stay here."

"I don't want you to go, either," I said. "I know you're fast and strong. But Lula, that does not make you invincible, love."

"I never thought…" She licked her bottom lip. "Ricky said Raven was right." She shifted the pillow under her head. "She said Dominick was turned by the monster who attacked us. I know killing him isn't our goal. I know killing him doesn't have anything to do with finding the monster who attacked us. Doesn't really have anything to do with finding the book and destroying it, which is what we should be doing."

"Or hiding the book," I said, "if we decide to believe what Raven was saying about Ordinary."

"Believe a god?" She slipped her hand forward and rested it on my hip. "Doesn't sound like us."

I put my hand on her back, the heat of her skin under the soft tank top warming my fingers. I pulled us just that small bit closer together and made a sound of agreement.

"So," I said, "I think we need to choose how we're doing this tonight. And whatever choice we make, we do it together."

"I can't walk away from saving that little girl. If there's a chance, I want to save her."

"I agree. And that means we do it together."

She hesitated. I could see how much she wanted to argue, how afraid she was for me. "I know," I said, even though she hadn't said anything. "I feel the same about you. We will keep each other safe. We'll trust that we can each take care of ourselves, right?"

She didn't look away, didn't frown. But I knew she wanted to argue a different way forward.

"Love." I tipped my head down so we were eye-to-eye. "I can't let you go into that vampire's territory, into that vampire's home, alone. It's just not in me."

"Brogan, if you're hurt…if you're killed…"

I shook my head. "I'm capable of staying alive, of being with you, no matter what tries to keep us apart."

"You have to promise me you'll remember you're human."

"I'm not human."

"Human enough." She lifted her hand and cupped the side of my face. "Promise me."

"I promise I'll remember I'm human. But trust me, love. There has not been a moment since Cupid brought me back to this flesh and bones body that I have forgotten it."

That seemed to settle something in her, and she rested her hand on my hip again. "Has it been difficult?" she asked. "You haven't talked about it."

"Haven't I? Feels like I'm constantly complaining."

She shook her head. "Is it worse being human than you remember?"

"Worse than before we were attacked by Atë's monster? That was so long ago, I don't know. No, not worse. I think it's better. Little things surprise me. I like that."

"Little things?"

"How soft a bed can feel. The smell of dew as the sun rises. You."

"Me?"

I hummed and brushed stray strands of her hair away from her face. "The silk of your hair. The scent of your perfume. Your lips."

Her pupils were wide, nearly eclipsing the ring of golden amber glow. "What about my lips?"

I hummed again, as if trying to remember what I was going to say. "Let me see…" I leaned toward her, closing the space, angling my mouth toward hers.

She shifted upward, her eyes fluttering closed, her lips soft, inviting.

My blood thrummed a heavy beat. Heat coiled and bloomed outward, setting my nerves on fire. Every sensation was magnified, the air too hot, too cold, the distance between her body and mine finite, endless.

I slid my hand under her shirt, caressing the lean line of muscle down her back, then drew my hand forward, tracing the curve of her breast with the back of my thumb.

She shivered. "Brogan?"

"Yes?"

She swallowed, opened her mouth, swallowed again, wordless. Then she was there, her mouth against mine.

We didn't need words, had never needed them to tell each other what we felt, what we wanted, what we needed.

I YAWNED and scrubbed the back of my head, glad the moonlight was bright enough I could see our very black dog as she poked around in the dry grass and shadows outside the honky tonk.

I'd gotten a couple hours of sleep before Lu woke me to shower and change.

We'd both agreed Lorde would be staying behind with the witches. We hadn't discussed our rescue plan, or how we intended to take out Dominick.

Lorde trotted over to me and bumped my hand with her nose. "Ready to go inside?" I asked.

She wagged her tail and started toward the front of the building. I followed behind.

The building was cooler inside than outside, but not by much.

They'd pulled back a false ceiling to reveal magic symbols painted on the wooden frame above the wall. An array of windows in the roof were formed in the stages of the moon cycle from new to full.

The moon wasn't quite overhead yet, but it still shone bright enough to bathe the bar in silver light.

The place was filled with people, everyone moving from one area to the other, like this was another kind of dance, weaving energy with soft chants and gestures, setting out crystals and herbs, bones and blades, and other offerings in a circle around the dance floor.

I knew just how much power this coven could tap into on that floor when they all worked together.

This time their focus would be to keep their land and people safe from vampire attack and also to cloak us while we moved inside the vampires' territory to find Rhianna.

I found an empty spot by the wall where I could watch, and parked myself and Lorde there.

Just a few minutes later, Lu strode into the room. She'd showered and put on black pants and shirt and braided her hair back.

The silver wing feather key hung around her neck on the same chain as the stopwatch, and the cloaking bracelet Ricky had given her was on her wrist. She'd strapped on her knives and hooked the explosive acorns into her belt.

She scanned the room, finding me, then strolled over. "Did I miss something?"

I shook my head and realized I'd been staring at her. "No. You look perfect." I opened my arms. "Me?"

Her gaze turned critical as she considered my loose, long-sleeve shirt, dark pants with the vampire-killing knife sheathed at my hip, and the ring that was supposed to give me speed on my finger.

"The spool of thread?" she asked.

I patted my pocket. "Unless you want to carry it?"

She shook her head. "Would you stay if I asked you to?" she asked, moving closer to me.

"Right next to you. Every step, love. I can't stay behind."

She pressed her lips together against the argument I saw in her eyes.

"We're going to be quiet," I said, "fast, and careful."

She stepped into my embrace.

"If you die again, Brogan Gauge," she whispered fiercely against my heart, "I will tear the heavens down to find you."

"Won't have to. Death won't let me in."

The embrace lasted just a moment longer, then she stepped back, adjusted the chain at her neck to hide the feather and watch under her shirt, and squared her shoulders.

Abbi appeared from out of the crowd, Cassia, resplendent in a flowing black gown that glimmered in the moonlight, beside her.

"We need to be really fast," Abbi said. "Really, really. The spell won't last long."

"An hour would be best," Cassia agreed. "We might be able to hold the cloaking for longer, but if you can find her and get her out in an hour, the spell will be strongest."

Hado, the tiny cat at Abbi's feet, drew up into the shape of a man made of shadows, his golden eyes glowing. He handed Abbi the mortar and pestle she used for her magic.

"You sure you don't want Abbi to stay here?" Lula asked. "To help support the spells?"

"I'll help them," Abbi said. "But I can help you too. If I stay here, it will be harder to help Rhianna."

"Thank you, Moon Rabbit," Cassia said. "And thank you, Lula and Brogan. Please bring our child home safely."

"We will," I said.

Cassia bowed to Abbi, then made her way back into the flow of people.

"Are you sure you shouldn't stay?" Lu asked Abbi again.

"I'm sure," Abbi said. "And you need me. Because

I'm powerful. *So* powerful! I'm going to be bright as the sun!"

"Nope. You can only be bright as the moon," I corrected her. "The sun is much brighter. Besides, we're trying to hide, Pumpkin, not be seen."

"I'm still gonna be bright. You'll see. Come on." She and Hado started toward the door where Variance was pacing and throwing glares our way.

The witches stopped milling around and gathered in the center of the room in a loose circle. They silently walked around the circle, once, twice, thrice.

Then they began singing.

The song rose slowly, a soft call and answer that whispered from the corners of the room, from the rafters, from the hidden spaces.

As more and more voices joined the call, as more and more voices joined the answer, the song became wind, the rustle of green and leaf, the twining of root and soil. Magic rose, humming in struck chords, gathering thick, strong, whole.

Silver moonlight met that magic and paled into neon pastel, a web woven upon light and song. The spell spread across the circle, shifting subtly, threads of light and sound pulling and knotting into an intricate spider's web above them.

The web lifted to the ceiling and hovered there, becoming heavy with moonlight that dripped like dew drops down each thread to the witches below.

Lula, next to me, was just as mesmerized at the show of magic. I reached for her, my hand extended palm down.

She, without looking, without seeing me, extended her hand, palm up.

We had done this for years. Me, invisible, her, unseeing. We had always known when the other was there. When the other was reaching out.

We clasped hands, and she looked over at me. I nodded, and together, we strode out into the night.

Franny was outside, wearing clothes that looked like she was ready to hike the badlands.

Abbi and Variance stood by an SUV with its engine running.

"Don't worry about Lorde," Franny said, as she opened the doors of the SUV. "Pru's going to look after her. She's wonderful with dogs."

"Thank you," Lu said.

"Shotgun!" Abbi called.

"No," I said. "Adults in the front seat."

I moved toward the front door, but Variance was already there, sliding into the seat and slamming the door behind him.

I scowled, but Lula tapped my arm. We took the center set of seats, and Abbi hopped into the seat in the back.

The car was spacious, modern, and aggressively cooled by the AC.

"How fast can you get us there?" I asked.

"Twenty minutes."

"I could get there faster on my feet," Variance said.

"Yes, but you aren't doing this on your own," Franny said, sounding every inch like an auntie who was not going to take any shit. "Because if you think you can dump the Moon Rabbit, or the Gauges, or me, Variance McClellan, you have another think coming to you."

Variance pulled his shoulders back.

Franny made an intricate sort of waggle of her fingers and a wave of exhaustion closed around me. It took everything I had to keep my eyes open.

"Enough," Variance growled.

Franny snapped her fingers, and the overwhelming fatigue was gone.

I was excruciatingly awake, as if I'd just downed a couple extra strong cups of coffee.

"I hate when you do that, Auntie," Variance said.

"Well, then. Stay in the car. Stay with *us*, Vari. It's going to take all of us to save her."

He didn't say anything more, so Franny adjusted the mirrors, revved the engine, and took off like a bat out of hell.

THE CITY of Amarillo had a population of just over two hundred thousand people. I didn't know how many monsters were in that town, but I did know Dominick's ranch could house dozens of vampires.

Dominick's vampiric call to battle was strong enough my headache was back, but otherwise, I could ignore it.

Both Lula and Variance had gone into that eerie stillness and silence only a supernatural could attain.

It was taking a lot more concentration and will for them to refuse that call.

Franny pulled the car onto the shoulder outside the city limits. Amarillo was still a ways off, sparkling in the distance.

A barbed-wire fence ran along the side of the road. Beyond that stretched dry ranch land dotted with scrub.

There were lights out that way, in a configuration that indicated they were from the ranch house. Other smaller lights around that cluster had to be outbuildings.

"I think I should go in with you," Franny said.

"No, you absolutely should not," Variance said before any of the rest of us could chime in. "There are already too many of us going—too many chances we'll be seen or caught. You're our way out, Fran. Our best way to get Rhianna home quickly and quietly."

I saw the conflict on her face, but she sighed. "I knew you'd say that. And you're right. You're right, Vari. I brought this in case she needs it to remember."

She pulled a little stuffed toy out of the door pocket. The palm-sized, lumpy beige thing might have once been an elephant, but it had been worn until it had lost an ear, a leg, the tail, and an eye.

Variance seemed to soften slightly, then he tucked the toy into his pocket. "Don't stay after dawn," he said. "If we're not back in two hours, go home, Franny. Get safe."

"I'll be right here when you come back. I'll be fine. We're bringing her back this time, Vari."

A flashlight beam flickered beyond the fence, three quick blinks, then three long ones.

"That's your inside man," Franny said. "Find Rhianna. Bring us Dominick's blood. Be careful. I love you."

Variance was out of the car before any of us had unbuckled our seat belts.

We quickly followed, but he wasn't waiting.

He'd already stepped over the section of fence conveniently broken and lying on the ground, and was making his way across the field, aiming toward where we'd seen the flashlight beam.

Abbi, with Hado in man form, bounded ahead of both me and Lula. We were right on their heels.

The flashlight flickered again, and Variance readjusted the angle of his approach.

The taste of dust kicked up by our boots filled my nose and mouth along with the pitchy scent of juniper and mesquite.

It wasn't just my headache. Everything about this mission made me queasy.

"How bad is it?" I asked Lula.

She knew I meant the vampiric call. "I can handle it."

"Are we trusting their inside person? Are they, like, a spy?" Abbi asked as she trotted to keep up with Variance's long stride.

"Only one way to find out," Lula said.

A figure walked our way. A man, I thought. Familiar.

He stopped a couple yards away from us, and we stopped too.

"Fuck, no," I growled.

The man—the hunter, Hatcher, who Lula had been sneaking around with— smiled. "Well, look at us now."

"The Hunter?" Abbi asked.

"The asshole," I answered.

"Both, yes," he said. He had traded his white shirt and cross necklace for plain, dark pants, boots, and a black shirt. He didn't appear to be carrying any weapons, but appearances could be deceiving.

"You're working with the witches?" Lula asked.

He nodded.

"Why?"

"Dominick has something of mine. A token. I want it back."

"Get it yourself," I said.

He shook his head. "It doesn't work like that. There are…limits to my capabilities."

"What capabilities?" I blurted. "You shot my dog because you missed shooting my wife. Given the chance, you sure as hell would have done more than that. You stole the damn book and sold it to the damn god who wants us dead."

"I was jumped. I lost the book before I could take it to my client."

"Who is your client?" Lula asked.

"We don't have time for this," Variance said. "We'll find your token, if you keep your promise to the witches."

"Like hell we will," I said.

"Headwaters," Hatcher said. "Headwaters hired me to look for the book. You found it before me in Illinois."

I blew out a breath. Great. Lula had been working for the mysterious magic and antiques collector for years. Now we find out Headwaters had sent a monster hunter to get the book, even if that meant killing Lula. Did that mean Headwaters was working for Atë?

"We don't need your help," I said.

"Fuck that," Variance growled. "I don't give a damn if you hate him, if he knows where my daughter is, we follow him and give him anything he wants."

"What can he do?" Abbi asked.

Yes, her voice was small, but she was a deity. It carried and silenced us all.

"I know our powers," she went on, her demeanor that of a mentor, an ancient. "What are yours, Hatcher?"

He shook his head. "First, I want the agreement sealed. I will help you save the child, *and* I will tell you where I've hidden the book. For that you will return the token to me."

"You just said you lost the book," I said.

"I stole it back when Cupid and Atë were fighting

in Oklahoma. Bring me my token. Then you'll know where the book is hidden."

"Fuck the book," Variance said. "I'll make sure you get your token."

"No." Hatcher didn't even look at him. "I want the promise from them."

Them, meaning us.

"Hunter," Abbi said. "What can you do? You will show me what you are."

Hatcher glared at her, but then his expression went slack. His eyes unfocused and his stance relaxed.

"Oh," Abbi said, "I see you now. Yes. We will retrieve your token in exchange for you telling us where you hid the book, and your help in rescuing Rhianna."

"Abbi," I warned.

"No. He can do this," she said. "He's important. Show them."

Hatcher shuddered as if he'd just felt a cold breeze, then took two steps backward, fear rushing his movements, his eyes narrowing.

Yeah, she was not what she looked like.

He stopped himself from outright turning and running. Whatever that token meant to him, it was enough that he would face down a deity.

He tipped his chin up at an angle, but kept his gaze firmly locked on Abbi.

Then he held his hand out toward Variance.

Variance drew a strand of hair out of his pocket. There was enough moonlight, the strand glittered silver. He gave it to the Hunter.

The Hunter dropped the hair into his mouth.

Between one breath and the next, the hunter was standing there.

Then he wasn't the hunter.

He was a little girl with Variance's eyes: Rhianna.

CHAPTER EIGHTEEN

Variance made a low sound and swallowed back a sob. Then silence filled the whole of the vast space as if the world had forgotten how to make noise.

"You're a ghoul?" I managed, my voice low, this child, hunter, monster, all I could see.

The girl nodded.

"Your shape," Lula said. "Does the token contain your original shape?"

Her guess surprised the ghoul. "Yes." Even his voice sounded like a little girl.

I might be angry, I might be a bastard, but I could tell that creature in front of me was telling the truth.

"If Dominick keeps the token, what happens to you?" she asked.

The monster child tipped her head down, as if even considering that possibility was unthinkable. But when she looked up, her mouth was twisted into a bitter anger no child would ever show.

"Parts of my form will disintegrate," the child said. "It will be agony. And it will lead to my madness and then my death."

I wanted all of that for Hatcher, for the creature who had tried to kill Lula.

But I wanted to save Rhianna even more than I wanted revenge. I wanted Variance to have some chance of returning to a human life so he could be her father.

"How do we know you aren't working for Dominick?" I asked. "Or for Atë?"

He shrugged. "You can't know, other than taking my word. But if you get my token, I will help you retrieve the girl."

"We don't have time," Variance said, his tone flattened as if it took every ounce of effort he had to speak. "Do you know where he's keeping her?"

"I do."

"Take us to her."

"If they promise to retrieve my token."

"For fuck's sake," I said. "Yes. Fine. Where is it? What does it look like? And why the hell does Dominick have it in the first place?"

"It looks like a coin," the ghoul said. "Dark metal, engraved. It was in Dominick's chambers. In a box."

"That doesn't sound at all like a needle in a haystack," I groused.

"The Moon Rabbit can find it," Hatcher said.

We all stared at Abbi. Behind her, Hado crossed his arms over his chest. She frowned. "I think I can. But you have to give me a strand of your hair."

The ghoul snarled, showing way too many sharp teeth for the little girl shape he was wearing.

"I see you, but I don't *know* you, Hatcher. Without something of you, your real form, I don't think I can find your token. Not fast enough."

"We have an hour," Lula said.

"Forty minutes," Variance said.

"At the most," Lula went on. "Give her your hair, or the agreement is off. We'll find the girl, and get the vampire's blood, and track down the book without you."

He said something in a language I didn't know, but he was not happy. Still, he plucked a hair from his head and held it out for Abbi.

It was thick and coiled and a deep, dark blue.

Abbi dropped it into her mortar and waved the pestle in a circle, staring into the bowl as if it held secrets of the universe. Hado put his hand on her shoulder, and the bowl flared a bright white-green. Abbi whispered to it, stirring the contents.

"You will get Dominick's blood," Variance said.

Lula nodded. "We will." There was more she wasn't saying. That she intended to kill the bastard as soon as we got that blood.

"Maybe Brogan can stab him," Abbi suggested, still staring in the mortar. "Like he stabbed Atë."

Heat from embarrassment, but also pride, burned beneath my skin as Variance and the ghoul stared at me with new consideration.

"Yeah," I said, my hand dropping to the vampire knife at my side, my gaze on the ghoul alone. "I can stab the vampire."

It was a promise I could stab other things too, like ghouls who had tried to shoot my wife.

"Oh, I can see the token now," Abbi said. "It's very pretty."

The ghoul made a small sound. "Are we agreed, then?"

Lula nodded. "We are agreed."

The ghoul's mouth did something between a grimace and a smile.

"This way," he said.

We jogged to keep up as he dashed across the dark field, the sounds of our bootsteps filling the still air.

"Where will Dominick be?" Lula asked Variance as we neared the house.

But it was not a house. No, we didn't have that kind of luck. It was a mansion.

"Dining hall," he said. "That's what they call it, but it's a throne room."

"Where is Rhianna?" she asked.

The ghoul child pointed to the left. "She should be in the outbuildings."

Variance growled and it made the hair at the back of my neck stand up.

"Captive," Variance spit out.

"They have cells there," the ghoul agreed. "It's a place they keep food. And betrayers."

"Is it guarded?" I asked.

"I'll deal with the guards," Variance said.

"If he's dealing with the guards," I asked. "What are you doing?"

The ghoul smiled and this time it looked exactly like child's glee. "I'm the distraction."

THE REST of the plan was argued over and filled out in short whispers and gestures. Vampires had good hearing. While we were still several yards out from the house, we very much did not want to be overheard.

The ghoul had supernatural speed. He would draw the guards' attention and pull them away from the cell where Rhianna was being held, allowing Variance to slip in and find his daughter.

"What happens if you're bit by a vampire?" Abbi asked the ghoul.

Hatcher clucked his tongue. "Not much. I'm already a monster."

So, that was one thing we had going for us.

"Who goes with Variance to retrieve Rhianna?" I asked.

"No one," Variance said. "I'll be faster on my own."

"Agreed," Lula said. "We're running out our time and magic, Brogan."

"I'll get the token," Abbi offered. "I know where it is."

It took everything in me not to argue that one of us would go with her.

But from the look on Lu's face, if one of us was going with her, it would be me. That wasn't going to happen. I was not going to leave Lula to face Dominick alone.

"But I won't be there to protect you," Abbi argued, as we all checked weapons.

Variance and Hatcher ran toward the outbuildings, their speed taking them into the darkness and out of sight in an instant.

"We have all the magic Ricky gave us." I dropped to my knees and tied the end of the spool of magic thread around Abbi's wrist. "The thread will help us not lose you."

"And me not lose you," she said.

"Exactly." I dropped the spool into my pocket. If I squinted, I could see the thread between us, but I felt no physical connection, no tension of real thread. It was magic, and the magic would connect us.

"I have the bracelet to cloak us," Lula said, "and Brogan has the knife that will stop the vampire dead. And I have the vials for his blood."

"And the bombs," I said, adjusting the ring on my finger and hoping the speed it would give me would be enough to keep up with Lula.

"And that," Lu agreed.

"Take this." Abbi held up a slick black feather.

Raven's feather.

"No, you need that," I said.

"Take it." She thrust it into my hand and took a step back. "We're all going to meet back at the road with Franny, right?"

I shoved the feather in my pocket. "Yes. Be careful, Pumpkin. If we aren't at the car by dawn, don't wait for us."

She scowled. "I'll go to the car, but I'm not leaving without you. We're family, remember?"

I reached for her and drew her against my side in a hug. "Of course I remember. Which is why I'm counting on you to keep yourself safe."

She nodded. "Hado will help me."

"I know he will." I released her.

Lula nodded. "Be careful, Abbi."

She nodded. "I'll race you," she said. Then she and Hado jogged ahead, closing in on the side door Hatcher had told us would be unlocked.

"Worst plan we've ever come up with?" Lula whispered, taking my hand so that the effects of the bracelet would cloak me too.

"Top three," I agreed.

It didn't take us long to reach the door Abbi had already slipped through.

It opened into what I assumed was a mud room, but it was set up like a lounge, with a bar on one side, a wall of closets on the other side, thick, expensive carpeting covering the floor, and an open archway into a second space straight ahead filled with lush, comfortable, heavy wood furniture.

Everything was done up in what I thought of as Texas chic: lots of animal skulls, a few human skulls sprinkled strategically among them, animal skins, leather, sticks and stone. All of it in shades of brown and white, with deep blue and deep red as accents.

Abbi was disappearing around the corner into the larger room, quick as a bunny.

The house felt empty, silent, as we crossed the mud room. The faint sound of country music played through speakers mounted in strategic places in the ceiling.

Waylan and Willie were telling mamas not to let their babies grow up to be cowboys. They had it half right—mamas shouldn't want babies getting turned into vampires, either.

Lu pointed left, and we crossed the lounging space to a smaller door at the end.

Into a wide hallway.

Abbi was nowhere to be seen.

We moved quickly down the hall, me keeping to Lula's pace with help from the ring.

According to Variance and Hatcher, Dominick's throne room was at the end of this hall.

It felt like this corridor went on forever, and that it would take hours to get to the end, no matter how fast we jogged.

I had a surreal moment trying to do the math for how many miles of carpet it took to cover this place.

I was sweating hard and working to keep my breathing under control.

Lu wasn't even breathing fast. She was focused, fluid, intent on the goal, on the task ahead of us. A killer waiting for her chance to strike.

Magic from the witches and magic from the bracelet cloaked our movements. We had as much of the element of surprise on our side as we could expect, but we still had to open the door to the throne room.

No matter how quick and quiet we were, there was a strong chance whoever was in there would see it open.

Lula mouthed, "*One, two, three,*" and pushed the door.

It swung silently. Lu slipped through the opening, me on her heels, closing the door behind us just as silently. We dashed to one side.

The light was low, but the first sense I got was that the room was huge, the size of two ballrooms, with way too many animal-antler (and human-bone) chandeliers hanging three stories down from the sky-lighted ceiling.

Pew-like seating spaces were built along the walls, interspersed with chains along the floor, shackles, leather straps and bindings.

It looked like a place where people would be judged and sentenced. It looked like a place where people were punished.

The space was huge, but it did not dwarf the throne on the raised platform in the center of the room.

A throne that held a vampire.

No, not a vampire. This was Dominick.

He was lean, long legged, and dressed in denim, a western-cut shirt, cowboy boots, and yes, a very expensive 100x Diameter Stetson.

His eyes were cuts of light, sunk deep and set too wide on his pale, flattened face.

But it was the child on her knees in front of him that stopped us cold.

Rhianna.

Dominick held a knife in one hand, casually rested across her slender throat, so that every time she swallowed a thin trickle of blood dripped down her neck.

He had been expecting us.

This was a set up. We'd been set up.

The child was breathing hard, her eyes showing too much white. She trembled with panic and fear that were too real.

We were screwed.

"I know you're here, prey," Dominick rumbled, his voice low, filling the room so it felt like I was breathing him in, swallowing the rot of him. He may not have been the monster who attacked us, but he was old, and terrifyingly familiar. "You will not leave this room alive."

Lu bit her bottom lip, scowling. We didn't have a backup plan. The plan we'd had—to sneak up on the vampire and stab him—was gone now.

Abbi was in the wind, searching for the ghoul's token.

I had no idea how long it would take Variance and the ghoul to figure out Rhianna was not in any of the outbuildings.

I had no idea how many vampires were between them and us.

I did know there was exactly one vampire in front of us who was ready to kill the child, kill us.

Fuck.

Lula squeezed my hand and twisted. Before I could react, she let go, leaving the bracelet circled around my wrist.

She grabbed an acorn and threw it.

An explosion rocked the other side of the room.

A wall of roses, stems as thick as tree trunks, thorns as long as scythes, burst through the impact point in the floor, rushing upward to punch through the ceiling and send wood and glass raining down.

The entire building moaned.

Dominick shot to his feet, pivoting toward the explosion, the knife in his hand, leaving the child (thankfully, mercifully) unharmed at his feet.

But Lula was still moving. She threw another bomb and sent another wall of vines and thorns rocketing from floor to ceiling.

Dominick hadn't moved, but he was tracking her. No matter how fast she was, he was faster.

He roared and lunged after her.

Rhianna curled into a ball, tucking her face into her drawn-up knees.

I hated what Lula was doing, hated this plan she had set into motion without giving me a choice.

But I was not going to fuck up our chance to save the girl.

I ran for her.

Another explosion deafened what was left of my

hearing while chunks of the ceiling hammered my head and shoulders with bruising force.

I skidded onto my knees beside the girl and pulled off the bracelet cloaking me.

"Rhianna. Hey, sweetheart, it's okay. I'm here to take you back to your Grandma Cassia."

She tipped her head just enough to peer up at me.

"Your grandma wants you to come home now. All your family wants you to come home now. I can take you to Franny who is waiting in a car. Ready?"

She buried her face back into her knees and shuddered as another explosion rocked the house.

I touched her shoulder and when she didn't react, I put the bracelet back on and scooped her up.

Vampire bit, I reminded myself. She was stronger than she looked, and faster, just like Lula. But she was still a child. A child who was in the middle of a nightmare.

She automatically wrapped her arms around my neck and held on.

I ran for the door we'd come in, stumbling over wood and plaster and stone, hoping I wasn't going to break my neck with the speed the ring gave me.

At the door, I glanced behind me.

Lula was locked in a fight for her life.

She was fast, though the vampire was faster, ruthless with her knives, though the vampire was more ruthless with his.

She was bleeding from several cuts on her arms and face. Her left arm hung at her side, useless. Dominick was toying with her now, it was obvious.

And I still had the vampire-killing knife at my side.

"Fuck all," I panted.

Why hadn't I given her the knife that would kill the bastard? Why hadn't she taken it from me?

She was going to lose this fight.

She was going to die.

CHAPTER NINETEEN

I have done some stupid things in my life. As a young man, as an earth-bound spirit, and as a man who'd almost-died too many times to count.

(Four. I'd almost died four times. It was countable, but I didn't like doing it.)

There was no chance I would be fast enough to take Rhianna to safety and get back in time to help Lula.

Even if she had the knife.

That didn't mean I wouldn't try.

I rushed down the hall, desperate for a door I could open, a safe place I could put Rhianna so I could at least get the knife to Lula.

Then a child came around the corner. A girl who looked just like Rhianna.

Hatcher.

Sometimes you have to trust someone untrustable.

I pulled off the bracelet.

He took in the situation and popped something

into his mouth. In an instant, he once again looked like the hunter. "I'll take her."

I had a slice of a second to make my choice. Did I trust him with the child? Would he hurt her, or would he take her to safety? He could just as easily betray us, betray the witches and Variance.

"I can run faster than you," he said. "I can get her back to the car."

"Where's Variance?"

"At the car. Injured." Hatcher glanced over my shoulder then back at me. "Badly."

Had he been the one who injured Variance, or possibly killed him? Had he been the one to tell Dominick we were coming to get the child tonight?

Or was he telling me the truth and he could get Rhianna to safety?

He snarled at my hesitation, then plucked a hair. "Here." He shoved the hair at me. "Now you have a piece of me. You will return it with my token. Go. Save her."

I didn't want to trust him. Everything in me said he was my enemy.

It would be easy to think he was working with Dominick and the vampires. That he wanted to kill Rhianna and send me in to fight the vampire so Lula and I would both be dead.

Trusting him might be foolish, but I could not leave Lula to die.

I tucked the hair in my pocket. Then I knelt, keeping my eyes on Hatcher, Rhianna balanced on my knee. I withdrew the spool of magic thread and tied it to her wrist.

"The Moon Rabbit is on the other end of this," I said. "If you break it, if you hurt the child, or if she dies, the Moon Rabbit will destroy you."

Hatcher shrugged. "I want my token, not a dead witch child."

I stood and handed the girl to the ghoul. She resisted but was too exhausted to put up much of a fight.

Hatcher was surprisingly gentle with her and made soothing noises as he adjusted his grip.

"Good luck, Brogan Gauge." He ran. Between one breath and the next he was gone.

The entire exchange had taken seconds.

Another explosion rocked the house. I braced my hand on the wall to keep my footing. How many bombs did Lula have? Five? Six? How many explosions had there been?

I slipped the cloaking bracelet on my wrist and lurched back toward the room. The oily perfume of crushed roses weighted the air, overpoweringly strong, burning my lungs.

The doorway that had been open moments before was now blocked by thick, dark vines studded with thorns.

"You've got to be kidding me."

Beyond the vines, I could hear the fight in the room, the labored grunts and thuds, the slap of boots on marble floor, the ringing of blades.

I pulled the vampire-killing knife and started sawing through vines.

With each slice of the magic blade, the vines shivered, cracked, and shattered like great glass icicles falling to the ground.

It took minutes, hours, forever, my thoughts whiteout panicked, my breath wheezing as I begged powers that had never listened to me to let her be alive.

Let her still be alive.

Then, finally, I could see them.

Locked in a deadly dance, Lu and Dominick moved so quickly across the room, I could only make out their forms when they paused or caught the other in a hold.

Even with the ring's speed and the cloaking bracelet, there was no chance in hell I could get close enough to stab the vampire and do any damage.

I reached into my pocket for the spool of thread. I needed to call Abbi, needed her to help me help Lu.

But there was no thread in my pocket because I'd tied it to Rhianna.

There was, however, a single crow feather.

Raven's feather.

I pulled it out of my pocket and held it up.

"Raven," I said, breathless, "get your ass over here. If she dies, I'll kick your shit to hell and back." I waited, my heart pounding.

Nothing.

"Fuck."

Dominick and Lula were on this side of the room now, about forty feet away from me.

The vampire backed Lula up until the thorny wall pricked through her shirt.

She was breathing hard, sweat plastering the hair that had come loose from her braid to her face. The cuts on her cheek, forehead, neck, arms, flowed with slow, dark blood.

Dominick had two wounds I could see: a slash down the side of his face that ended just short of his jugular, and a wide gash across his stomach. Neither of the cuts bled freely, even though the wounds were deep.

Vampires were hard to kill. A couple cuts wouldn't do it. The only reliable way to end them was a stake through the heart or beheading.

"Enough," Dominick said, the command thick with disappointment, scorn. "You bore me, *thrawan*."

Lula bared her teeth, gripping her blood-covered blade. It was not a blade that could kill the vampire.

I had that blade in my hand. I balanced it between my shaking fingers, holding it like a dart. This was a foolish idea. It was stupid to throw a weapon, to bet it all on one wild chance.

The blade was heavy, not meant to be thrown this way.

I was a good shot, but hitting a vampire who could move faster than the eye could see? Those odds were south of nothing.

Dominick shifted his grip and drew back to plunge his knife into Lula's heart.

I threw the dagger with everything I had.

"Hey!" I yelled, dropping the bracelet so I was visible.

Dominick pivoted, Lula twisted…

…and the dagger I'd thrown stuck, center of the vampire's chest.

Dominick roared and scrabbled at the dagger, his knife dropping from his fingers.

He turned on Lula, but she had put distance between them, limping out of his reach with her good arm across her stomach, her eyes shocky and wide.

He got his hand on the hilt of the knife in his chest, trying to pull it free. He roared again…

…and hundreds and hundreds of crows filled the room.

The birds dove through the holes in the ceiling, winged in from the hall, from doors that burst open, from cracks in the floor.

Cawing, shrieking, diving with sharp claws, tearing with wicked beaks, the crows surrounded him, a melee of talons and sound, tearing into him as if he had stolen and eaten their young, wanting him shredded and dead.

I was already running to Lula, blinded by black wings. Not a single claw struck me as birds wheeled away, clearing a path.

I caught only glimpses of Lula through the flash of black feathers, like a movie skipping frames.

She was still on her feet and limped forward toward the shrieking mob of birds that covered the vampire.

She held a blade in her fist and inhuman hatred in her eyes.

"Lu!" I yelled, but my voice couldn't pierce the fury of the crows.

I was almost there, almost close enough to help her.

But Lu didn't stop. She swung her blade in a tight arc, her whole body rocking with the effort. The blade sliced a path exactly where the vampire's neck should be.

The birds burst away from Dominick, painfully silent now, just the whispered brush of feathers stroking the air.

They rose upward, a spiral, a black tornado of clever gold eyes and hushed wings funneling out through the broken ceiling, casting into the night as if they had been nothing but smoke. Nothing but dream.

Dominick screamed, a feral beast of a sound, and lurched, arms outstretched.

Lula was too close. Too damn close. He grabbed her by the neck, sharp nails digging in.

She shouted and struggled backward.

Then the vampire's head rocked sideways and fell off.

Lula shoved at his body with her good hand, and he slumped to the floor.

I crossed the final distance to her, just as she turned toward me.

Her expression was fierce, then worried as she took me in, then relief washed over her.

"Brogan," she breathed.

I wrapped my arms around her, and she leaned into me, taking all the weight off her left foot, nearly collapsing.

"Love, love," I babbled, fear and adrenalin making my thoughts too fast and my movements too slow.

"I'm okay, I'm okay," she chanted against my shoulder. "We have to go, we have to go. His blood."

She withdrew a small vial from her pocket. She pushed away from my hold and tried to bend to get some of the vampire's thick blood into the vial but gasped in pain.

"Here, here now." I took the vial from her and knelt by the body.

It was more difficult than I expected to get the blood off the floor, to get it into the glass tube. It was thick and slippery and shifted away from the edge of the glass.

So, I changed tactics and shoved the tube into the mess of vampire flesh. I moved the vial around until the viscous fluid filled the tube, then pulled it out and stuck the stopper in it.

"Are there more vamps?" I asked. The knife I'd thrown was still sticking out of his ruined chest. I retrieved it and sheathed it at my side.

"I don't know." She swayed slightly. From the dilation of her pupils, I suspected she had a concussion. "I can't hear them."

"Can you walk?"

She nodded, took a step, hissed.

I caught her up, one arm under her legs, the other across her back. "This will be faster."

She went stiff, resisting, then used her right hand to pull her left arm up into her lap. She rested her head against my shoulder.

I was strong, and Lula, being *thrawan*, was surprisingly light. I moved as quickly as I could and as quietly, stepping over broken vines and shouldering sideways through the long, sharp thorns.

If Hatcher was telling the truth, there were more vamps around here. Without the magic string, I didn't know where Abbi was or if she was still looking for the token.

"Can you sense Abbi?" I asked.

Lu lifted her head. "I can't hear her. I can't feel her. Rhianna?"

"Hatcher took her to the car. I tied the string to Rhianna. Maybe Abbi followed it and is already with them."

"I can walk," she said.

"Once we're out of the house. Watch my back."

Lula stared over my shoulder as I stepped out of the room.

The hall was empty, the proportions of the building out of whack, the hallway stretching out endlessly.

Adrenalin was a firehose in my veins. I wanted out of here. I wanted out now. If I could have snapped my fingers and called a god to transport us to the car, I would have done it, no matter the price to pay.

I was trying not to run. I couldn't be so pushed by fear that I missed a possible danger.

The place might be filled with vampires. Every corner, every door, every room.

Sweat ran down my back. I shifted my grip on Lula. There were no vamps in front of us. There were no vamps behind us.

I paused outside the sitting room.It looked exactly the same as when we'd come through what felt like hours ago. Country music murmured from the speakers, a song about love being a butterfly.

No vamps in sight.

I strode across the room and into the mud room. No one there either.

"Put me down," Lula said. She held on with her good arm, and I released her legs. She stood, most of her weight on one foot.

"Ready?" I asked, my hand on her hip steadying her.

She nodded, her knife low.

I opened the door. Warm night air peppered with juniper brushed my skin. Still no vampires.

I knew our luck wouldn't hold. We needed to move fast. I bent to pick her up again.

"Brogan, you don't have to—"

"I carry you, or you ride on my back. You can't run, Lula. Not on that foot."

She scowled, but pointed at my shoulder, then sheathed her knife. "Your back. Your hands will be free."

I turned and crouched.

217

She gripped my shoulder and hopped up. She wrapped her legs around my hips, her left arm tucked between us, her right holding on tight.

"Good?" I asked.

"Good."

I straightened and walked into the night.

The moon hung high and full, silver light shellacking the land around us and washing out all but the strongest of stars.

I started across the field, dust kicking slow-moving eddies around my boots. I was still sweating, but the fear had eased off enough I could hear myself think. It didn't make sense that there had been no other vamps in the house.

Had Variance and Hatcher drawn them all away? Had they killed them, or injured them enough, they couldn't come to Dominick's aid?

"How far?" Lu asked, words slurring.

"Not far." It was a lie. The meeting point at the car was at least a mile away.

Even with the ring that gave me greater speed, carrying Lu and picking my way between scrub and over broken ground was slowing our progress.

Lu stiffened and tapped my shoulder. I stopped. "Vamps," she whispered, her lips so near my ear, I felt the word more than heard it.

I released my hold. She slid off my back and pulled her dagger. I drew the vamp knife. "How many?"

She didn't have time to reply. Dozens and dozens of figures melted out of the darkness, surrounding us.

There wasn't time to plan. There wasn't time to strategize. There wasn't time to call for help or find an escape. The vampires were viper-fast, attacking with teeth and blades, too many, too fast.

Lula fought like wildfire, her blade flashing with moonlight and blood as she parried strike after strike.

I slashed and blocked, stabbing eyes, open mouths, necks, using my bulk and reach to guard her as best I could.

If a vampire fell, another was instantly in its place. We would not win this fight. There were still too many, there had always been too many.

A body slammed into me, carrying me down. I hit the ground, air whooshing out of my lungs, my head bouncing off a stone.

The world swam, and I wanted to puke. My reactions slowed to a snail's crawl.

The vampire above me was darkness and pain, I lifted one arm to block the bite…and then…then it collapsed on top of me and was still.

Good: I hadn't been bitten. Bad: I couldn't move.

I needed to find Lula. I could hear her still fighting but couldn't see her. I blinked and almost fell deep into that soothing darkness before forcing my eyes open.

The moon was huge, filling the sky. It burned my eyes, bright and brighter, blotting out my vision, so bright it could almost have been the sun.

Then, impossibly, the moon shone even brighter.

The vampires screamed.

"I see you." A voice—Abbi's voice—carried the

power of her magic. "Beneath my light, you are ash, you are dust. My magic is acid on your skin, it is poison in your veins. I am brighter than the sun. You will not thrive in my light. You will not live."

She said something else, a stream of syllables I couldn't understand, and the night grew even more painfully bright, as if a bomb had just gone off.

The screams grew louder.

Then there was silence.

Then there was darkness.

"Lu?" I whispered. The weight holding me down was gone, but I still couldn't move. I tried lifting my hand, a finger.

Nothing.

A hand cupped the side of my face. Lula. I knew her touch, would always know her touch. Her fingers drifted across my lips.

The lips were the last part of the body that could feel sensation before a person died. I'd read that somewhere. I wondered if it was true.

"I can't see," I said.

"It's okay. It's okay."

"I love you," I told her, as I always would.

"I love you," she answered, as she always did.

The darkness pulled away as my eyes finally adjusted.

Lula sat above me. There were more cuts on her face, a bruise across her temple. She looked pale and haggard. She was still the most beautiful thing I'd ever seen.

"I told you I was bright," Abbi said from behind Lu.

Abbi looked much older, her mouth set in a grim line, her gaze hard and angry. Hado behind her was a massive black cat, prowling, gold eyes burning like flames in the night.

"You weren't supposed to tie me to Rhianna," Abbi said. "I could have been here faster. I could have found you faster and burned all the vampires faster."

I tried to sit, but the world spun. Lu pressed on my chest. I gave up and stayed where I was.

"I knew you'd find us," I told Abbi. "Because you are magic like that."

She tipped her head, looking at me through narrowed eyes. "Because we're family."

Then there were more hands, as Franny helped me sit. "Here now," she said, passing me a bottle of water. "Drink slowly."

Lula stood with her own bottle of water and drank it while keeping an eye on Hatcher.

The hunter moved from body to body, studying their faces, then gathering hair from some of them.

I polished off the water and, ignoring the warning look from Franny, pushed up to my feet. My head hurt, and I'd be feeling aches and pains for days, but I could walk.

"Where are Variance and Rhianna?" I asked Franny.

"I took them home for medical attention. I'm here to take you all back."

"No one leaves until I get my token," Hatcher said.

He came closer, still in the shape of the hunter we'd first met. I didn't know much about ghouls, but he looked just as dirty, tired, and bruised as the rest of us.

"Where's the book?" Abbi asked.

"Where's my token?" The hunter looked at her, then at Lula and me.

Abbi opened her palm. In it was a small coin, carved symbols around its edge, and in the center, what looked like a human standing by a fire.

"You don't want to lie to me," Abbi said clearly. "I can kill you."

The hunter met her eyes. He'd just witnessed the power she had called upon to kill the vampires. He had to know she could absolutely back up that threat.

"I buried it," he said, addressing her, then me and Lula in turn. "In Adrian. The midpoint of the Route. There's a windmill there. It's beneath it."

That was about fifty miles west of here. There were a lot of windmills there. I couldn't believe it was that close.

"How do we know that's true?" I asked.

"We'll keep the token until we have the book," Lula said.

"That's not what we agreed on," he argued.

"It's what we're doing," I said. "We'll meet you at the windmill in Adrian tomorrow night. Before sunset."

The hunter wanted to argue, I could see that. But

I was feeling better, Lula looked ready for a fight, and Hado loomed over Abbi and snarled.

It was Franny who broke the stalemate.

"You have traded fairly," she said. "I give you my word and the bond of my coven. We'll see to it they meet you there before sunset, with your token, which we will guard and keep safe.

"Also," she said, "if you need medical care, healing, or rest, we will provide it for you. You are welcome to return with us."

I didn't think I'd ever seen the real face of the ghoul before.

But for a moment, he was so shocked by that offer, his entire face seemed to shift into something that almost looked like longing.

Then he shook his head as if warding off an annoying gnat.

"Tomorrow," he snarled. "By sunset. If you betray me, I will hunt you down and feast on your entrails." He took one step back, two.

Then he was gone, faded into darkness.

Abbi blew out a breath. "Okay," she said. "We need to go back to the witches now. Right? We're going back?"

"We're going back," I agreed.

Lula put her hand on Abbi's head, and the Moon Rabbit leaned her face into her side for a minute.

"Thank you," Lula said. "You did really good."

"You were bright," I added. "Like the sun."

Abbi held still a moment, then tipped her head up.

"I'm getting cookies for this, right?" Her mouth dipped then rose again like she was fighting off tears. "Or ice cream?"

Abbi wasn't a fighter, wasn't a killer. She was good at running and hiding. She was good at seeing things and hearing things.

But she'd just taken on a swarm of vampires and melted them down like she was the sun itself.

"You get all the cookies and ice cream you can eat, Pumpkin," I told her.

And oh, the smile she gave me.

CHAPTER TWENTY

I fell asleep on the car ride back to the honky tonk. Abbi woke me and Lula both. The witches were at the door, helping us out of the SUV and into the bar.

Rhianna, with the ratty little elephant toy clutched tightly against her chest, was already showing signs of being more human—her color better, her eyes less hollow.

Cassia carried her off to a room, singing a sweet lullaby about pretty horses.

Variance was on a stretcher in the middle of the dance floor. He'd been bathed and bandaged and was asleep. Several people gathered closer to him and picked up the stretcher, following Cassia out of the room.

If they were lucky, if they mixed the spells correctly with the vampire blood, Rhianna would be fully cured.

"We're hopeful for Variance too," Franny told Lu

and me, as she led us back to a bedroom. "The spells from the Crossroads were very powerful. We will return them once they are both healed."

The room was small, painted a soft green, and was very clean, smelling of gardenia. A queen-size bed, with a carved wooden headboard and patchwork quilt, filled most of the space. A door at the end of the room led to a small, private bathroom.

I wanted to fall onto that bed and sleep for a century.

"I'll send Cassia in to look at your injuries," Franny said. "You can shower if you want. There's water there," she pointed at a minifridge, "and I'll bring you some food. Lula, do you need blood?"

The offer was so natural, so casual, you'd think she'd been cavorting with vampires all her life.

But then I remembered Variance had been here, living with them since he'd been turned vampire. They must have figured out some way to look after his nutritional needs.

"I don't—"

"Yes," I said. "That would be good."

Franny nodded and let herself out of the room.

"I could have answered," Lu said.

We hadn't moved any farther into the room. I thought we were avoiding the bed for fear we'd get into it and never get out.

"I know." I took her hand and looped it through my elbow so I could help her to the bathroom. "But you would have said no."

"You think you know me so well?" she teased.

She was exhausted. We both were. And this—talking about nothing, arguing about nothing—was keeping our minds off of sleep, keeping our minds off of what we'd be doing tomorrow.

Finding the book and dealing with the troubles it brought with it.

"Oh, I do know you," I said. "For example, I know your birthday is tomorrow."

She stopped and tugged on my arm. "You remember that?"

"Of course I remember that. I've wished you a happy birthday every year of our lives."

Not that she could hear it, all those years of me being without a body, without a voice.

"I like that," she said. We started moving again. "I've wished you the same."

"I know." I opened the door and whistled in approval.

The bathroom had a large shower with a wide rainfall fixture, a bench in the shower space, and a large bath outside the shower space. Several soft-looking towels waited on floating shelves.

"You first?" I asked.

"There's room for both of us." Then she tugged me toward the shower.

I got busy getting the water to temperature, while Lula pulled off her clothes. She had regained a little more movement in her left arm, but it still wasn't fully functional. I stepped over to help her undress.

She stilled, letting me take my time drawing off

her tank top, then easing the straps of her bra and undoing the hooks.

I untangled the band from her braid next. She shivered as I drew my fingers through her hair.

Next were her boots. The small bench near the bath let her sit so I could unlace and pull. Finally, her pants.

By the time she was standing there, naked in front of me, the room had warmed, steam filling it, softening the air.

I drew my hands down her arm and ribs, one hand pausing to cup her breast.

"Lu," I breathed, wanting her. Wanting to feel her alive in my arms, wanting to trace every inch of her, to feel the silk of her body, her thrumming heartbeat.

She held her breath, then exhaled in a soft laugh. "We reek of vampire," she said. "Clean. We both need to get clean."

She touched the side of my face, then limped into the shower.

She was exhausted. Injured. I was too.

I shucked out of my clothes and thought boring thoughts to calm my body's natural reaction to her. I stepped into the shower, and she pulled me to her, inviting me into the water.

So much for keeping my body in control.

I shifted, fitting us better together. She placed her hand on my arm to help steady herself, not being able to put weight on her left foot. Since her good hand was helping keep her steady, she was out of options for soap application.

"A little help?" she asked, nodding at the shampoo.

"Happy to oblige."

I poured soap into my palm. It smelled like gardenia too. I worked it into a foam and pulled my fingers over her scalp, then scrubbed the soap down through her hair.

She hummed and closed her eyes, leaning her face into my chest. I washed her hair, reached for more soap, then took my time washing her body.

She winced more than once as I sluiced soap and water over her back and ribs. Among her cuts were several bruises, one spreading across the top of her foot and up her ankle and calf.

I guided her to sit on the bench while I soaped myself down, hissing as it stung multiple nicks and cuts.

The lump on the back of my head was sore and felt bigger. I washed my hair, soaping up several times until the water didn't run as red and the cut had gone numb.

Lula watched me the whole time, her eyes like honey in water.

She liked what she saw. But exhaustion carved shadows into her, and I was fading fast.

"Bed," I said. To her raised eyebrow, I added, "Sleep."

She bit her bottom lip but nodded. "Tomorrow."

I grinned. "Always."

We dried. We'd forgotten to take our clean clothes into the bathroom, but when we opened the door to the bedroom, our duffles were waiting on the floor next to the bed.

Lorde was lying right in the middle of the bed, facing the bathroom.

She *woof*ed softly and whined, her bushy tail wagging.

"Hey, girl," I said, as I reached her and scrubbed behind her silky soft ears. "Did they look after you? Give you treats?"

She panted and licked at my face, then did the same when Lula sat on the bed next to her.

I found our comfortable clothes. Lula and I put on the essentials and crawled under the covers, Lorde smooshed into the narrow space between us.

I was already half-dozing when the knock on the door startled me awake. For a moment, I couldn't remember where I was.

Lorde stuck her big head on my chest and breathed dog breath into my face, and it all came back to me.

"Come in," Lu said.

Franny and a woman with short yellow hair that curled around her head stepped into the room.

"Food," Franny said, indicating the platter she carried with a couple bowls of soup and a plate piled with fried chicken, mashed potatoes, and green beans.

"I'm Trella," the other woman said. "I'm a nurse practitioner. I need to look you both over. No, it's fine. Just stay there. I can get to both sides of the bed."

Franny put the tray on the bedside table next to me, and I could see I was wrong about the bowls.

They didn't hold soup, they held a couple cups of blood, the red stark against the fine white of the china.

"Hungry?" she offered me.

My mouth watered from the delicious smell of chicken and potatoes, and my stomach cramped. "I am now."

I sat, and she produced a lap table and set up the plate for me, then looked over at Lu. "Food?"

She nodded. "Yes. Thank you."

She repeated the process with her.

Trella worked around us while we ate, and didn't seem even slightly distressed that Lula was drinking blood.

"The ankle is a bad strain," she said, her hands careful on Lu's foot. "Let's get some ice on it and elevate."

She got busy doing that, and I lost myself in some of the best fried chicken I'd ever put my teeth into.

Trella narrated our injuries: *bruises, stitches, rotator cuff strain, slight concussion, bruised ribs,* while moving to apply the fixes as she talked.

The doctoring went a lot faster than I expected, though I might have lost track of time while cleaning off the plate.

Franny took the empty dishes and made sure we had water on both sides of the bed. Then she and Trella left.

Lu was lying on her back, her foot propped up on pillows, an icepack wrapped around her ankle. She had needed a few stitches and butterfly bandages, but there wasn't much to do for the bruised ribs or strained rotator cuff other than to put her left arm in a soft sling.

I'd gotten my share of stitches—more than her—but Trella assured me my concussion wasn't too severe for me to sleep.

Lorde had refused to leave the bed, and now that they'd left, she wormed her way back between us.

I'd meant to ask about Variance and Rhianna, I'd meant to ask if Abbi was okay.

But Lula was already breathing deeply and evenly, the soft sounds of music and voices in the main bar a pleasant ocean of white noise. She reached for me, resting her hand on Lorde's back. I lifted my hand and threaded my fingers through hers.

Lorde sighed and made a happy grumbling sound. We slept.

SOMEONE WAS STARING AT ME.

I opened my eyes.

"Hi," Abbi whispered. "Are you awake now?"

It took me a second. "Uh."

She leaned back in the chair she'd pulled next to the bed.

"I think you're awake now. It's morning. But morning is almost over. Do you want breakfast or lunch? Oh! Or breakfast *and* lunch?"

I rubbed a hand over my face, trying to scrub thought back into my brain. "What time is it?"

"Almost lunch," she said. "I've had cookies, and cake, and a donut. No, two. Two donuts."

I rolled my head to look for Lu. She sat on the other side of the bed, the pillow propped behind her back.

She'd re-braided her hair and was wearing a clean, soft yellow tank top and a pair of shorts.

She looked like sunlight and sweet water.

"Morning," I said.

"Afternoon," she replied. "I'd go for lunch. They're making up more of that chicken you fell in love with last night."

I gave her a look. "I was hungry, not proposing to it."

She flashed me a smile. "Well, there's still a chance, since it's for lunch. Plus fries."

It sounded delicious, but I wasn't about to let her know that. "Maybe I want breakfast."

"Do you?"

"That's not the point."

She smiled. "Cassia wants to see us. For lunch."

"I think there's more cake!" Abbi bounced in the chair. "Or maybe a pie. I like pie."

I wanted to tell her she needed to maybe eat a vegetable this year, but she wasn't human and could probably eat anything she wanted.

"I need to get dressed," I said.

"Oh, good! I'll tell Cassia we're staying for lunch." Abbi hopped off the chair and flew to the door, throwing it wide. "He says yes! We get to stay for lunch! Can I have pie?"

The door swung shut behind her and closed with a solid click.

"It's like living with a hurricane," I said. "How are you feeling?"

Lu tossed her braid behind her shoulder and leaned down to kiss me. I didn't know what she was expecting, but I held her there, my hand coming up to cradle her head. She melted into the kiss, and I never wanted it to end.

When we came up for air, her pupils were dilated, and her mouth was pink, a blush of color warming the freckles across her cheek.

"We have witches to talk to," she said softly.

"Mmmm." I reached for her again.

She evaded my touch. "And a book to recover."

"Mmmm."

"And," she said, getting off the bed and walking with a much smoother gait than last night—one good thing about her being a *thrawan* was that she healed quickly—"a ghoul to meet."

I put my arm behind my head, showing off the bulge of my bicep. "Bed's comfortable. Maybe the witches can wait."

She took in the show and waggled her eyebrows. "Sooner we're on the road, sooner we'll have a new place to stay for the night. Who knows what will happen then? It is my birthday, after all."

With that, she slipped out the door.

Birthday. I had wanted to throw her a party. I had wanted to give her gifts and her favorite dessert. I had wanted her to feel spoiled and special and treasured.

None of that had happened, and I'd run out of time.

I sighed, pushed off the blankets, and grabbed clean clothes. By the time I was pulling on my shirt, I had an idea.

It took me several minutes to find where I'd stashed it, and I kept glancing at the door hoping Lula wouldn't walk in.

The demon stone was wedged in a pocket of my duffle. I hadn't put it there.

Abbi might have, but I had the feeling demonic items put themselves wherever they wanted to be found.

It was a huge risk to do this here among the witches, but the only way out of the room would mean passing the bar. From the sounds drifting in through the door, there were plenty of people out there, which meant I couldn't sneak away.

I held the stone in my palm, took a few deep breaths, then quietly spoke.

"Bathin, if you're listening, this is Brogan Gauge. You gave us this stone to use if we needed it. If we needed you. I didn't want to use it. I don't want to make a deal with a demon. But I have a proposition for you."

By the time I had carefully—very carefully—laid out my idea, about fifteen minutes had passed. Nothing had changed in the room. I had no idea if the demon had even heard me.

If he had, I wasn't sure he would agree to the terms I had laid out.

But I was out of time. If I lingered any longer, Lu or Abbi would get suspicious and come looking for me.

I tucked the stone into my pocket and walked to the bar.

Sunlight filtered through the windows, but the honky tonk was cool, the ceiling once again covered by solid wood, the air-conditioned breeze good enough it could make one think Texas heat wasn't all that bad.

There were a lot of people from the coven here, the neon OPEN sign switched off.

Lu sat with Abbi and Cassia at a table to the right, so I headed that way.

"Have a seat," Cassia said. "Hope you don't mind we ordered you up a lunch."

Since the lunch was fried chicken, ribs, a good helping of beans, and fresh steaming corn bread, I plunked down into the chair.

"It looks amazing, thank you."

Lula lifted her iced tea and took a drink. The bowl of fresh fruit in front of her was half empty, strawberry stems and little strips of melon rind left in a pile on her napkin.

Abbi, to my surprise, was eating a peanut butter and jelly sandwich. "This is my second one," she said.

Cassia didn't have food in front of her, but she did have a large earthenware mug steaming with a fragrant tea.

"I'd leave you all to your meal," she said, "but first I'd like you to fill me in on where things stand. Franny and Variance have already told me what they know. Abbi explained what happened on her side of things."

"I stole the token and killed the vampires. Because I'm really bright." That last was a challenge to me.

"Meh," I said, "you're bright enough."

"Like the sun!"

"Sure, bright like the sun." I pinched my fingers to indicate she was a little bit short. "Almost."

Her eyes went wide in outrage, but it was spoiled by the dab of jam stuck on the corner of her mouth.

"Who wants to be the stupid sun anyway?" she muttered, taking another bite. "The moon is so much better."

"If you can," Cassia went on, "please tell me what happened when you got to the vampire stronghold. There are a few pieces missing from the story."

Lula took the lead, which gave me some time to mow through half the food on the plate.

I *was* hungry, but I'd eaten a big meal last night and found myself slowing down to listen to Lula recount the fight with Dominick.

"And then there were crows," she was saying. "I think…Brogan? You were a part of that?"

I took over, explaining why I'd given Rhianna to the ghoul, and how I had guaranteed her safety.

"I like the part when you tell him I can smoosh him like a bug," Abbi said.

"Then I went back for Lula. To fight Dominick. The vines…" I shook my head. "I had to hack through them to even get into the room. I had the vampire-killing knife Ricky gave us." My hand drifted to it at my hip. "But I was too far away, and too slow."

"Like I told you," Abbi pointed out.

"Like you told me. I dropped the bracelet, threw the knife, and yelled to get his attention."

Cassia and Lula wore matching frowns. Yeah, I didn't need either of them to tell me how stupid that had been.

"It struck true," I said a little more defensively than I liked. "His heart, or near enough. But it didn't kill him. Lu was hurt, I was weaponless. I found Raven's feather in my pocket, and I asked for his help."

"The crows," Cassia said. "He must have sent them."

I drank coffee. The witches really knew how to make a mean cup. It was rich and delicious.

"It was enough," I said, "the crows hurt him enough, distracted him enough, blinded him—that Lula was able to cut off his head."

That was simplifying it a bit and leaving out the part where he'd tried to choke her to death, but those weren't details I needed to share.

"He died," I said. "I filled the vial with blood from his still twitching body—does that make a difference for your spells?"

She shook her head.

"I filled the vial, and we left as quickly as we could. We were about halfway across the field when the vampires surrounded us."

"At this point," she said, "you only had your daggers?"

"That's right."

"I wasn't at my best," Lu admitted. "My injuries slowed me down. Slowed us down."

"I slowed us down." I pointed at my face. "Human." I pointed at her. "More than human."

"But you fought them?" Cassia pressed.

"We fought them," I said. "We weren't going to win that fight."

"Then what happened?" Abbi asked with a big grin. "Did something amazing happen? Did *someone* amazing happen?"

"Then," I said, "Abbi shone her magic. And she was bright as the sun."

"Yes!" She threw her hands in the air and tipped her face to the ceiling. "Bright as the sun! So bright I melted the vampires!"

Hado, in kitten form, on her lap *meow*ed.

She looked down at him. "Okay, also I used a lot of magic, which probably did most of the melting."

"After that, we made the deal with Hatcher to return the token in exchange for the book," Lu said. "Franny was there."

Cassia sipped tea then nodded and set the cup down.

"The blood of the vampire, combined with our magic and portions of the spells in the book from the Crossroads, has been very powerful," she said. "We were able to use it to return Rhianna to her human self.

"She's sleeping, but we expect a full recovery. We're still doing what we can to reverse Variance's vampirism."

"Can you do it?" I asked, keen to know if they had some way to help him. Keen to know if they could help other people who were bitten.

I glanced at Lula who stared at me, knowing what I was thinking. Could her bite be reversed? Could she become human again?

"Because Variance's bite is so recent, because it is the blood of the vampire who turned him, and that vampire is now dead, yes," Cassia said, "I think we can. But it will take more time, more magic. A lot of patience."

"If he'd been bitten a longer time ago?" I asked. "Say several years ago?"

"No, I don't think we'd be able to change that, to change him." Her gaze shifted to Lula. "I'm sorry."

Lula relaxed. It had been a long shot, thinking the witches would know a way to return her to her human self.

"I'm glad for him," Lu said. "For both of them."

"Please stay with us awhile," Cassia said. "You've done so much for us. We will help you keep the book safe and hidden, and if it comes to it, we will stand with you against the gods."

I was stunned. It was an incredibly generous offer. And an incredibly dangerous thing to offer. I didn't have to look at Lu to know we were of the same mind, but I did anyway.

"Thank you," Lula said. "That's very kind of you.

But we will not bring more trouble and pain upon you and yours. We can't."

Cassia looked like she was going to dig in for a long argument.

"I'll look after them," Abbi said. "They'll look after the book. We're going to be okay. I promise."

Cassia sat back and tapped her finger on the tabletop. "The offer still remains. If you need sanctuary, we will give it."

"Thank you," I said. "If we need your help, we'll reach out."

"Good," she said. "Let us pack you food and any other supplies you might need. We have a box you might be interested in taking with you. It can hide even the most powerful magic."

"Is it big enough to hold a book?" I asked.

She nodded. "Plenty. Moon Rabbit?" she asked. "Would you sit with us one more

time for Rhianna and Variance?"

Abbi slid off the chair, and rubbed her sleeve over her mouth, wiping off jam. "Sure."

Cassia stood, and Lula and I rose with her. "Thank you," she said, taking first my hand, then Lu's. "Blessed be."

I felt the strength of her words and the magic, both carrying the silken song of light and moonlight and leaf.

She and Abbi crossed the dance floor.

"Thank you," Lula said, coming around the table to me.

"For?"

"Asking."

"About?"

"Variance. His bite, his cure."

"We'll find the answer," I said.

She shook her head. "It's been a long time. I don't know…don't know if we can find that answer. Or if I'd want to change." She tipped her chin up, her eyes a challenge.

Huh. I hadn't ever thought that she wouldn't want to be human again. That she might like being what she was now, that she was comfortable in who she was after all these years.

"If that's what you want," I said, "then we won't look for the answer. I love you, Lula Gauge. As you are, as you were, as you will be."

She placed her hand over my heart. "I might want to have the answer. To know the answer—even if I don't do anything with it."

"That's good too."

"Thank you," she said, her eyes sparkling with sunlight.

This time, I answered with a kiss.

CHAPTER TWENTY-ONE

It was hot as the devil's armpit, and even with the windows of the truck cranked down, there was no relief.

Lorde was at my feet on the floorboards, snoring. Abbi sat closest to the window, her arm stuck out, her hand flat so she could fly it up and down in the air current.

I sat next to Lu, my arm over the back of the bench seat, my fingers gently brushing her shoulder.

The radio played a country song, just loud enough I could catch the higher notes over the wind in the cab. The sun burned in the pale blue sky, lowering toward the horizon, but not yet giving in to the sunset, to the end of its daily rule.

If it hadn't been a thousand damn degrees outside, it might have been a nice, sleepy sort of drive.

If we weren't headed to meet a ghoul, who had tried to kill us, to retrieve a book that everyone else wanted to kill us for, it might even have been almost a perfect stretch of road.

Lula slowed the truck as we reached Adrian, the open fields with short square farmhouses, metal outbuildings, tall cylindrical grain silos, and rows and rows of modern windmills indicating people had settled here to build lives. This stretch of highway was smooth concrete, and recently painted with a huge white Route 66 shield right in the middle of the road.

The Midpoint Cafe and Gift shop sat on our left, the sign with the googie arrow pointing cheerily at the small, one-story white building that housed the home-cooking, 1950s-style café. It shared the parking lot with a brick motel on one side and a boarded-up gas station on the other.

There was only one car in front of the café, and it was not the hunter's truck. Lu parked in front of the building and turned off the engine.

"I'm going too," Abbi said.

I reached across Abbi to open the door. "We know. You've been telling us that for the last three miles."

"Because I have the token."

"Yep," I said.

She picked up kitten-Hado and dropped him on her shoulder where he draped himself. "And I made the deal."

"Part of it," I agreed.

Abbi shimmied out of the truck and batted at her yellow skirt to make all the folds fall the right way down to her knees. She wore a sparkly light blue tank top, and green socks.

"You look like a dandelion," I said.

She grinned at me. "Thank you! Cassia gave me this skirt. It swirls!" She held out the skirt and did a little twirl.

Lu stepped out of the truck. An oversized blue handkerchief covered her head in a triangle tied behind her braid. She wore a light linen, long-sleeved shirt, jean shorts, boots, and sunglasses.

I'd never seen a more gorgeous sight in my life.

She walked to me, and a smile lit up her face.

"So, what you said this morning," I said.

"What did I say this morning?"

"That it's your birthday."

"I recall."

"I'd like to do something special for you."

"Oh?"

I grinned.

"How special?" she asked.

I caught her hand and stepped close enough to breathe in her perfume. I leaned down, my mouth near her ear. "I'll show you later."

She made a dismissive sound, but her cheeks had gone pink, and it wasn't from the sun.

We started across the road, heading to the small windmill set a few feet back from the long, low wooden Midpoint of Route 66 sign (put there so people driving the Route could take photos of themselves in front of it).

They'd built a nice flat brick area for the sign,

giving folks a place to walk around that wasn't on the road or the farmer's field behind it.

The small windmill was the old-fashioned kind with a wooden base and small metal blades. There wasn't enough wind to turn the blades, not even with evening headed our way.

"There are a lot of windmills out here," Abbi said. "How do we know which one he meant?"

"It's the small one," I said.

"How do you know?"

"It's closest to the Route."

I scanned the area. Other than the distant squat buildings and telephone poles, the only other structure was a billboard built on the ground next to the intersection. It currently advertised where to turn for the nearest gas station.

As we walked toward the small windmill, a figure moved out from behind the sign.

Hatcher. The hunter. The ghoul.

He'd gone back to the dark denim pants, white shirt, black vest and necklaces. He looked the same as he had when we'd first seen him.

I figured he had a gun somewhere handy. I would if I were him.

He moved our way, close enough to be heard, but not close enough to be in punching range.

"You're early," he said.

"Not by much," I answered.

"Where's the book?" Abbi asked. She was on my right, Lula on my left.

He nodded toward the windmill. "Buried there. I've dug it up."

Lula strode toward the windmill. As soon as she was close enough to see the lump at the base of it, the hunter spoke. "Stop there."

He drew a gun, but didn't aim it at anything but the ground.

Lula stopped. "I need to touch it to know if it's real or not."

I didn't like this bit of our plan, but Lula was right. She was the only one besides Hatcher who could touch the book. If we'd traded places and the book was the real thing, I'd be knocked out cold the moment I got a finger on it.

"Where's the token?" he asked.

Abbi stuck her hand in her skirt pocket and pulled out the coin. "I have it. You know it's real. You can feel it."

He paused, as if testing her statement, then nodded. "Bring it to me."

"Lula gets to touch the book first," she said.

He swallowed and I thought for sure, he was going to argue. "Do it," he ordered Lula.

She strode the remaining distance, her mostly healed ankle only slightly shortening her stride. She bent and pressed one finger into the shadow beneath the windmill.

The thrum of energy, of magic, of god power was sub-audible, rolling through the land beneath my boots and ringing through my bones like a strike of metal.

It wasn't unpleasant. But it was god power, and I'd spent nearly a hundred years doing my best not to attract gods, or their power. I didn't like it.

"Okay," Abbi said simply. "I'm going to put this token on the bricks right here." She pointed at her feet. "You should put the gun away. Remember how I melted the vampires? I can make ghouls into goo too."

He returned the gun to the holster. "My hair," he said to me.

I held up the single strand he'd given me and which I'd managed not to lose.

Lula picked up the book and wrapped it in the handkerchief she'd had on her head.

"Put the token down," the ghoul said, as Lula strode our way.

Abbi did, and then took three exaggerated giant steps backward. "I told you I'd give it to you if you were telling the truth."

"This is yours too." I stepped forward and placed the hair next to the token.

Lu was at my side, then past me, headed toward the truck.

"You too," the hunter said to me. "Step back."

I took several steps backward, keeping my eye on him.

He darted forward, uncannily fast. He bent, scooped up the token and hair.

"We're done now," I said, holding my ground only a few yards from him.

He narrowed his eyes and looked past me at Abbi

and Lula. There was calculation in his expression. I didn't know if he was working out the risk of trying to kill us or trying to steal the book again.

"All of this," I said. "Done."

I wasn't magic. Not like the witches. Not like Abbi. But Ricky had told me, hell, Raven had told me, that I was the voice that could speak the spells in the book, just as Lula was the hands that could hold it.

Between us, we could wield the power of the gods.

It was the thing neither of us had spoken of yet. The very idea too large, too dangerous, too horrifying to try and quantify and accept.

But it wasn't the book that made me who I was. As Ricky had said, when I was without a body, when I was nothing but a spirit, I had had the power to affect the world, to use my voice to break through the walls that divided realities.

I put some of that into my statement, my words as precise and holdfast as nails hammered into stone.

The ghoul sensed it. Enough that he nodded. "It's done."

He turned and strode away across the field. His truck was parked in the intersection, and he piled into it and took off south down the gravel road.

I waited until he was out of sight. Only then did I turn and walk to the café parking lot where Lula, Abbi, and Lorde were waiting for me.

"All good?" I asked them.

Lula nodded. "I put it in the box the witches gave us."

"With my extra magic keeping it secret," Abbi added. She was rubbing Lorde's head.

"It's as secure as we can make it right now," Lu agreed.

"Good." I glanced at the café. "How about we get dinner before we find a place to stay?"

"We have a cooler full of food," Lu said.

"Sure. But a hot meal won't hurt us."

She frowned, and I thought I'd pushed it too far.

"They have pie!" Abbi skip-ran to the door, Lorde at her side.

"Can my dog come in?" she asked, standing outside the door she'd opened with just her head stuck into the place. "She's really hot."

There was a murmur of a male voice, and then Abbi shooed Lorde into the building.

"Looks like we're having dinner," I said.

"Looks like."

I gestured her to go first and followed her to the café.

She opened the door and stopped on the threshold. "Oh."

It was more than I had expected. More than I could have hoped to do on my own. Better, too.

The café was original to when it was built, which meant it had the markings of a place that had seen a lot of years. But the checkered floor shone, and the tabletops were clean.

Yellow and pink and green balloons, all tied together with shiny ribbons, floated above three tables that had been pushed together in the center of the room.

Hung across the wall was a huge banner that looked like it was made of silk with hand-stitched embroidery that read HAPPY BIRTHDAY, LULA. Twirly bits of crepe paper and other glittery gewgaws finished off the party decor.

A beautiful bouquet of flowers centered the table, and next to that was a pink frosted, strawberry angel food cake.

There were exactly four people in the room, and not one of them were people: a Moon Rabbit named Abbi, a trickster god named Raven, a demon named Bathin, and a Crossroads named Ricky.

They all wore shiny, pointed party hats. Abbi blew a noise maker, making the paper tube snap out and roll back.

"Happy birthday, love," I said.

Lu turned and pulled off her sunglasses. I was surprised to see tears in her eyes.

"Hey, now, are you…" I started to ask.

She reached up and kissed me. "Thank you," she whispered against my lips.

"Can we have cake yet?" Abbi asked. "Oh, no, we have to do candles first, right, Ricky?"

"That's the tradition," Ricky said.

"Lula, Brogan," Raven said, "come on over and have a seat. The birthday girl gets the tiara."

Yes, it was strange to have a god at a birthday party.

Yes, I had asked the demon for a favor. This favor.

Yes, I knew I would pay some sort of price for it. Demons never did anything for free.

But the joy on Lula's face, her laughter when I put on the extra pointy hat, and she put on the tiara, was worth it.

So was her delight at the gift from Crow—a crocheted bracelet with bits of glass, agates, and seashells dangling from it, and the gift from Bathin: ALL SYSTEMS RED, a book he insisted was worth reading because the robot was the best character.

Ricky gave her a quilt, made of floral fabrics, that she had hand stitched with green embroidery thread. Lula hugged her long enough, they both got a little teary-eyed.

Whatever price the demon would set for me to pay, it would be worth it.

"Open mine next," Abbi produced a box wrapped in paper she must have gotten from the witches.

Lula looked absolutely glorious in her tiara and tank top. She took the present and opened it carefully, savoring the moment. She lifted the box lid.

"It's a rock," she said.

Bathin, who was leaning on the counter drinking a cola, leaned forward, interested. "Ah." He leaned back.

"It's not one of yours," Abbi admonished. "It's a lucky rock. I found it by the Blarney stone. And since you didn't have a chance to kiss it for luck, I got you this pebble, which has to have some of the luck in it because it's like a baby Blarney. So now you can kiss it."

Lula smiled. "It's wonderful. Thank you." Then she made a big deal of giving it a loud smack, and Abbi clapped her hands.

"Time for cake?" Ricky put a pretty, yellow and white candle into the center of the cake.

"Lu?" I asked.

"Yes!" Abbi said. "Let's do cake!"

Ricky placed the cake in front of Lu.

Bathin lit the flame with a little snap of his fingers (showoff), and then we sang the song wishing her a happy birthday.

It's a short, simple song, but our voices seemed to make the best of it, Raven going for fancy harmony, Bathin carrying the tune with a warm baritone, Ricky's rich alto guiding us all, and Abbi's voice sweet and pure.

I was singing, too, my gaze on only one person, one woman. My life, my world.

Lula was crying, but the tears slipped almost as an afterthought into the corners of her smile.

She was watching me, too, as if this moment was one she would hold safe and secret to unpack again and again in the years to come.

I wanted that. I wanted that for her, and for me, and for us. Years and years of birthday songs. So many that the memories and the cakes and the wishes on candles all blended together into a blurry happiness.

"Make a wish," I whispered after the song was over.

She closed her eyes. We held the space for her, the silence, to give her wish its fullest form.

Then she opened her eyes and blew out the candle, giving the wish breath, life, wings. Her gaze found mine, and there was a question there, a hope.

Yes, I said, even though I didn't know her question. *Always, for you.*

She wiped at a tear with the back of her hand.

"Thank you," she said to all of us. "This is lovely."

"Wait until you try the cake," Bathin said. "Made by a friend of ours. He runs a bakery called the Puffin Muffin."

"You didn't make it?" she asked Ricky.

Ricky shook her head. "None of this was my idea. I love it, though."

"What kind of cake is it?" she asked, as Ricky handed her a knife and she cut off a generous slice.

"Strawberry angel food," I said.

"That's right." Bathin took the next slice and sat at the table. "Just like you asked."

Lu paused in cutting. "You asked Bathin to do this?"

"He had already used my feather," Raven said, like that had any bearing on the event. "I mean, what else are demons good for?"

"Ask me for a favor," Bathin said around a mouthful of cake, "and you'll find out."

"I'd rather work out the details later," I said. "And just enjoy cake now."

"Details?" Bathin asked, his gaze locked on me. "What details?"

Shit. This wasn't something I wanted to do in front of Lu. I had hoped to negotiate the payment for this in private.

"I assume you are going to set a price for putting the party together for me. I assume we will negotiate that after the party."

Bathin grunted and went back to eating cake.

"Thing is," he said, like this was a conversation he had been thinking over for a while, "demons are made for deals. We are transactional creatures. Self-centered too."

Lu placed a plate with cake in front of me, a little of her joy subdued as she listened to Bathin.

I grinned and took a bite, trying to keep the mood light. The burst of flavor and soft pillowy crumb melted in my mouth.

"Damn." I glanced at the demon. "Is your friend a magician? This cake is stunning."

He nodded. "Hogan does good work."

Lula made a humming sound, agreeing whole-heartedly as she sampled a bite.

"But I have a stake in this business now," Bathin went on. "In the two of you taking the book some-where safe. Ordinary, Oregon, is safe."

I wanted to ignore him and devour the cake, but I put the fork down and waited for the other shoe to drop.

"There are a few other places in the world that may also be safe," he said. "Safe from gods. Safe from demons, the self-centered transactional lot of us. But Myra's library in Ordinary is the safest."

He scraped the tines of his fork across the plate, gathering up the last of the bright red strawberry preserves.

"I don't like that book," he said. "I don't like what it can be used for. So, for the low, low price of one private birthday party out in the middle of nowhere, I want your promise that you'll bring the book to Ordinary, as soon as you can."

"Yes," Abbi agreed.

"You can't promise for them, Bun Bun," Raven said, sneaking Lorde bits of bacon that had appeared in his hand. "They have to make the deal with the demon themselves."

"Okay, but I still say yes."

"Why do I think it's a trap if I agree to this?" I asked.

"Because," the demon pushed his plate away and sat back, holding another full bottle of cola in his hand, "I'm a demon."

"Lying, cheating, self-centered, transactional, cruel…" Raven listed.

"Sometimes," Bathin agreed. "Not all of those things always. Not all of them this time."

I shook my head. We'd made promises to Cupid, made deals, and remade deals. The last thing I wanted was to tie us up in another promise with another powerful supernatural.

But what had I expected when I asked a demon to throw my wife a birthday party? I was lucky he wasn't demanding our souls for it, although our souls might be damaged in ways a demon wouldn't care to have them.

"Brogan," Lula said. "Can I talk to you a moment? Outside?"

"I'll make sure there's still cake when you get back," Ricky said.

"But we get seconds, right?" Abbi asked. "There's so much left!"

Lu and I walked out into the heat. The sun had slid toward the horizon, and though the heat was about the same, the light was richer, gold instead of piercing white.

We paused at the front of the truck where a little shade had inched out from the building.

An RV pulled off on the other side of the road, and six people who looked like three middle-aged couples all got out. They laughed, slapping hands in high fives, and strolled over to pose in front of the Midpoint sign.

"You asked a demon?" Lula said. "Really?"

"It's the first birthday I've had with you since the attack. I couldn't let it go without giving you a party. Without telling you how special you are to me. Without thanking you for waiting for me, all these years."

She just stared at me. I fidgeted, wiping the back of my neck.

"So, you called a demon?"

"I admit my planning could have been smoother."

She pressed her hand over her eyes. *Smoother*, she mouthed.

When she dropped her hand, I expected her to be angry. I was angry for making such a foolish decision, for putting what I wanted—a party for her—ahead of all common sense that one should not ask minor favors of major demons.

"You know we have promises to Cupid we are bound by," she said.

"I know."

"You know Atë wants to kill us."

"I know." I took her hand. "I wasn't thinking about all that. I was just thinking of you."

Having no personal autonomy for so many years had made me yearn for the ability to choose to do a thing, even if it was a foolish thing, and experience it being done.

"The cake?" she asked.

"Ricky and the Crossroads remembered it was your favorite."

"It really is marvelous. The best I've ever tasted."

I nodded. "Apparently there's a baker named Hogan in Ordinary who we owe some thanks to."

She shook her head, but I saw forgiveness, or at least acceptance in her smile.

"Did you invite Raven and Ricky?" she asked.

"I think Raven just shows up wherever he wants. I don't know how Ricky found out. Maybe he told her."

"You're welcome!" Raven yelled from inside the building, loud enough we could hear him through the windows.

I couldn't help it, I laughed. A moment later, Lula laughed too.

"So?" I said. "Do you like it? The party? The balloons and flowers?"

"I like the party. The balloons, the flowers, the cake. But mostly, I like you, Brogan Gauge. Thank you for the best birthday of my life."

I nodded, surprised at the wave of emotion that rose up to threaten tears.

"Let's go promise a demon we'll get the book to the library in Ordinary," she said.

I squeezed her hand, and we walked into the café, together.

EPILOGUE

Clouds came in with the night and the wind shifted, restless, in the slightly cooler air.

The moon, large and bright, drifted lazily behind the slow-moving clouds. The sky was riveted with pinprick stars, making it a lovely night for sleeping outside.

Abbi had declared the cab of the truck was now a tent fort and had stolen all the extra blankets and towels to turn it into a cozy little space.

She had also informed Lu and me that we were not allowed. Lorde was allowed. So, she and the dog and Hado, in tiny kitten form, were tucked up front, Abbi giggling and Lorde softly barking now and then.

Lu and I sat on the tailgate of Silver, our legs swinging, the quilt Ricky had given her across our laps. Franny had packed us beer, and it was cold, the outside of the bottle wet from melting ice.

I rubbed my thumb over the label absently, staring at the land, the sky, the huge horizon all around us.

"They could have taken the book," Lula said.

"Raven and Bathin?"

She hummed. The book was still stored in the box the witches had given us. It was in the bed of the truck, locked in the metal tool case we'd put behind the driver's seat.

Did it feel secure?

No.

Did it feel powerful?

Strangely, also no.

I didn't know if it was the witch spells, Abbi's spells, or just the fact that the book had chosen us, chosen Lu to be able to touch it, chosen me to be able to speak its spells—not that I ever intended to do such a dangerous thing.

But maybe now that it had gotten most of what it wanted, it was doing what it could to keep itself hidden.

I mean, it'd been hidden for years beneath a collapsed shed back in Illinois. I supposed it could stay hidden in our truck.

Wouldn't that be a nice change?

"They said they can't touch it," I said. "Raven went on about how it would break some sort of rule of him being on vacation. Whatever that means."

She turned the bottle between her fingers, thinking. "Trickster god and a demon."

"Demon prince or king, or something," I said.

"Demon prince or king," she corrected. "Are we going to trust what they say?"

The next shot of beer went down like ice and

electricity, hitting my stomach hard and spreading out a different kind of warmth.

"Agreeing to take the book to Ordinary doesn't break our promise to Cupid," I said.

"He'd want us to give it to him."

"Unless he doesn't," I said. "He's a god. He might already know we have it. Might not want to be more involved unless he has to be."

She took a sip of beer and leaned a little closer to me. I put my arm down behind her back and pulled her in.

"He knows where we are," she said.

"I assume so."

"When he comes to get it, will we hand it over?"

"We'll decide that when he comes."

"I think Raven and Bathin are telling the truth," she said. "About Ordinary. I think they might be telling the truth about the library. Ricky does too."

I hummed and tipped the bottle and took another gulp. I agreed.

She leaned her head on my shoulder.

"Party was really good," she murmured. "That cake."

"That cake," I agreed. We had about a quarter of it left, carefully wrapped and stored in the cooler. I had a feeling we'd finish it off at breakfast if Abbi didn't try to steal it in the middle of the night.

"Thank you," she said.

I tightened my arm to hold her closer and took another drink.

"Oh." She pointed at the sky. Between the break

in the clouds, a bright star burned as it shot downward.

Moonlight spun like soft silver across her face, making her glow. "Make a wish, Brogan Gauge."

"I already have," I said. "It came true."

"Me?" she asked.

"Always and only," I said.

Her smile was filled with love, yes. But even more, it held hope for good days ahead, and if we were very, very lucky, a life we could live, happily ever onward.

WANT TO READ MORE FROM DEVON?

Find her latest books and fun newsletter at her website:

www.devonmonk.com

ACKNOWLEDGMENTS

This book would never have come about without the contributions of so many talented people.

I'd like to give a huge shout-out to my amazing cover artist, Ravven, who not only nailed the cover for this volume, but also went above and beyond to update the first three (wonderful) covers of the series. Thank you!

To my fabulous copy editor, Sharon Elaine Thompson, thank you for your sharp eyes and for pointing out the rough spots that needed fixing. I appreciate you more than you know.

To my husband, Russ, thank you for that terrific road trip down Route 66, and for stopping in Shamrock to smooch the Blarney Stone—I love you. And to my kiddos, Kameron and Mike, Konner and Anna (and Phoebe!) thank you for letting me be a part of your life, I love you all.

Patreon readers: Aleta Goin, Anne Tisdale, and TJ Thornton, you rock! I am so grateful for your support!

And finally, to you, dear readers. Thank you for riding down the Route with Brogan and Lula and the crew. Until we meet again, safe travels, and happy reading!

ABOUT THE AUTHOR

DEVON MONK is a USA TODAY BESTSELLING fantasy author.

Her series include Ordinary Magic, Souls of the Road, Broken Magic, House Immortal, West Hell Magic, Allie Beckstrom, and Age of Steam. She also writes stand-alone novels such as Nursery Crimes, and the occasional short story which can be found in her collection: A Cup of Normal, and in various anthologies.

She lives in lovely, rainy Oregon and when not writing, she is drinking too much coffee, watching hockey, or knitting ridiculous toys.

ALSO BY DEVON MONK

Wayward Devils

Wayward Gods

Wayward Vows

WAYWARD STORIES
Oak and Ink

LAS FABLES MYSTERY
Nursery Crimes

HOUSE IMMORTAL
House Immortal

Infinity Bell

Crucible Zero

WEST HELL MAGIC
Hazard

Spark

ALLIE BECKSTROM
Magic to the Bone

Magic in the Blood

Magic in the Shadows

Magic on the Storm

Magic at the Gate

Magic on the Hunt

Magic on the Line

WAYWARD DEVILS

SOULS OF THE ROAD - 4

DEVON MONK

ODD
HOUSE
PRESS

For my Family--and all the dreamers on the road

Magic without Mercy

Magic for a Price

AGE OF STEAM

Dead Iron

Tin Swift

Cold Copper

Hang Fire (short story)

SHORT STORIES

A Cup of Normal (collection)